er

Here Comes the Miracle

'I adored this novel. Very lovely'   Pandora Sykes

'Incredibly moving. An original and powerful novel that looks to depict, in searing detail, the year from diagnosis to death of a terminal illness . . . There are echoes of Kate Atkinson's *Life After Life* and *A God in Ruins* . . . As with Atkinson, Beecher is interested in the choices people make and the emotions that prompt action . . . Her debut recalls the lyrical exploration of loss in Max Porter's *Grief is the Thing with Feathers*. Kit de Waal's *The Trick to Time* is another recent comparison, as is Sarah Winman's *Tin Man*. How we're shaped by the people we love is a central preoccupation of all these novels . . . *Here Comes the Miracle* may be a story about loss but it is also a testimony to life, survival and the revitalising powers of memory' *Irish Times*

'What a gorgeous book. Lovingly told, with a poet's eye for the small miracles to be found in each passing moment. Such light and poetic prose, at times unspeakably tender. There were so many moments I found incredibly moving'
                    Charlie Gilmour, author of *Featherhood*

'Powerful, sensual, deeply moving . . . A stunning novel I read in two evenings'
                    Clover Stroud, author of *The Wild Other*

Here Comes the Miracle

Anna Beecher

WEIDENFELD & NICOLSON

First published in Great Britain in 2021 by Weidenfeld & Nicolson
This paperback edition published in Great Britain in 2022
by Weidenfeld & Nicolson,
an imprint of The Orion Publishing Group Ltd
Carmelite House, 50 Victoria Embankment
London EC4Y 0DZ

An Hachette UK Company

1 3 5 7 9 10 8 6 4 2

Copyright © Anna Beecher 2021

A CIP catalogue record for this book is
available from the British Library.

ISBN (Mass Market Paperback) 978 1 4746 1064 3
ISBN (eBook) 978 1 4746 1065 0
ISBN (Audio) 978 1 4091 8646 5

Typeset by Input Data Services Ltd, Somerset

Printed and bound in Great Britain by Clays Ltd, Elcograf S.p.A.

www.weidenfeldandnicolson.co.uk
www.orionbooks.co.uk

For John

Joe

1987

You were born a bluish scrap, too small and too early.

You were placed in a plastic box, with holes in the side for adult arms to reach through. There you lay, unfinished, beside other babies, ventilators inflating rows of tiny lungs, names given in the hope of a chance to use them. A puppy, born tiny and lifeless, can be put into the oven on a low heat, where it will lie on the shelf like a chicken breast. Just sometimes it will come to life.

It was March. The corridors were briefly blasted with light. Fathers and mothers – men and women who had recently painted rooms in gentle colours and assembled new furniture – came and went with spring rain on the shoulders of their coats, while their babies bathed in the regulated, seasonless warmth of the incubators. They were sometimes allowed to sit and carefully slide gloved hands through the incubator holes, and sometimes put out into hallways to stand, staring at nothing, crushing plastic cups between their palms.

In the single photograph from this time, our parents, Ruth and Mark, look grave, despite the camera prompting the reflex to smile. They sit together on plastic chairs by your Perspex shell. A family portrait taken hastily in case you did not survive.

It is a cliché to call it a miracle, but that must be how it felt when it came. The bright room, the tubes that had punctured your fine, translucent skin, the educated, efficient people who stood at your side and wrote things down, the bag of a stranger's blood and the screen that relayed your fast, fragile heartbeat – these things had delivered you. After four days, you were moved to a different cot, one without a lid, one that you could easily be scooped out of and held, breathing for yourself, light but solid. And after a week, you were taken home in a blanket.

I think our parents almost forgot that it might have been different. Forgot the even tinier babies, red like skinned animals, their eyes fused shut. When those children were finally held, were their families glad it had been that way – their sons and daughters born and not miscarried – because there would be proof they had existed, birth certificates and graves?

At home, Mum took out the blue-handled scissors, cut the plastic bracelet from your wrist and put it away in a shoebox, so that she could take it out sometimes, read the name – *Joseph* – which had not been wasted, and marvel that any limb could have been so small.

Edward

1952

A hand reached through a gap in the hedge. Bitten finger-nails and a scar in the centre of the palm. A boy slipped his body into the space: the stretch of scrub between a shoe factory and a wood. A hidden place broken by a stream. Nettles rose up the banks and water licked around glass and reeds, the occasional half-made shoe. The boy was seventeen and taller than he'd like to be. High bones in his face, his hair almost black. A stripe of light crossed him. His name was Edward Blood.

He had discovered the place by accident, two months before, while searching for shelter from a rainstorm, and since then had gone there most days, pausing on his cycle home from school to walk down to the end of the skinny path or crouch on a log, reading in undisrupted solitude. But today, for the first time, he was not alone. He had hesitated to share the place, and now, as his friend followed him through the hedge, Edward tried to adopt a casual stance, scoring a crack in the earth with the edge of his toe. Jack was shorter and clumsier than Edward. The sun touching a few strands of his hair, he grabbed the leaves in handfuls and struggled to pull his bike through.

Once, when Edward was a little boy, his sister, Agnes, had caught a frog and told him to hold it, passing it into his palms and clamping her hands round his so he couldn't release them. The creature had pulsed in the cage of their fingers. Edward suddenly regretted bringing his friend here. What if Jack thought secret places were for children?

But Jack looked around like he had entered a cathedral, casting his eyes up to where branches broke the light. His gaze travelled over the treeline and the water, his mouth slightly open. What straight teeth he had. It was rare for Jack to be quiet. He laid his bicycle on the ground beside Edward's then straightened up, smiling. Jack had recently started to shave and there was a cut on his face and a tiny patch of stubble beneath his jawline. Edward brought his fingernails to his mouth, then remembered he was trying to stop the habit.

'I'll give you the guided tour,' he said, and turned, beginning down the path.

The narrowness forced them into single file, and behind him, Jack immediately began a rush of speech. Edward smiled and stopped listening. The roots that contoured the path felt pleasant through his shoes. He was in front, leading for once. He wondered what his back looked like.

'Right through his hand,' Jack was saying, 'blood everywhere.'

It was a story he had told before – the man in the factory who had punctured a lace hole in his palm.

Turning, Edward said, 'It can't have gone straight through.'

'It did. My dad was there when it happened.'

Edward batted a fly away from his face with an upward

4

gesture and Jack switched topic: 'You look like Mr Howard.'

Edward grinned, repeated the motion, adding a swipe downward and across – *up, down, right, left* – as if conducting. Mr Howard had recently arrived and taken over their school choir. His voice filled the room. His predecessor, Mr Jones, was a short, ancient man with tight, contained gestures and a shake in his voice. When he sang examples, he hurried through them or got one of the boys to do it. The first time Mr Howard opened his mouth to sing, Jack kept his eyes forward but pressed his elbow into Edward's side.

'No,' Jack said now, 'more like this!' He closed his fists emphatically, moved them through the air, then dramatically flared his fingers.

They were used to hearing, *A little more control, boys*, but Mr Howard told them all to stop holding back their voices. *You have to do both*, he said, *control it and let it out*. He told them to breathe into their ribs, not their throats, and made them place their palms between their waists and armpits to understand the difference. It made Edward think of the wide, curving ribs of cows.

Edward glanced down and spotted the white threads of Jack's shoelaces lying in the dirt.

'Your laces, Jack.'

Jack didn't move, so Edward crouched before him and picked up the threads, a crust of mud on one of the nibs. Memory of his mother saying, *Ears of the rabbit, round the tree, into the rabbit hole*. He had never tied another person's laces. He finished and looked at the shape of Jack's feet on the ground. A worn part in his white plimsolls at the knuckle of the big toe. The foot straining to get out. *What if I never get up?*

When he stood, their faces were close. There was a little sour note in Jack's breath. Wind through the leaves. Jack smiled at him. A corner-of-the-mouth smile. A mole interrupting his lip.

'How long,' Jack said, 'can you hold your breath?'

Edward hesitated. 'I don't know.'

Jack stepped forward and said, 'Let's see.'

'Like a game?'

Jack laughed. 'If you like.'

He placed his fingertips on Edward's shoulders.

Memory of a bomb. Not a real one, but pieces of an old motorbike Edward had found with his sister near their farm, the scattered parts rusting into the ground. Agnes had made it into a game, and they had circled it, sweat in her fringe, her eyes intense. *Careful, Edward!* He was seven then and games could still suddenly shift and feel real. She said, *Let's touch it*, and they crept up slowly. Fear ran hot through him as she held his fingers to a curve of metal arching out of the grass.

'First, we have to synchronise,' Jack said, 'then we'll take a big breath together and see who can hold it longer.'

They made their breaths audible until the in and the out were in time. Edward kept forgetting that he was allowed to blink. Then Jack took his fingers from Edward's shoulders and touched them to Edward's throat. He told him to do the same.

'So we'll know exactly who lets go first.'

If someone had stumbled upon them, they might have thought the two boys were engaged in a strange fight, slow and silent, both with a hand at the other's neck.

'Ready?' Jack asked.

Snake through time and find Edward somewhere else. Two months from this moment, his mother will sit beside him on his bed. He will think what thin eyelids she has, what a thin, small mouth. She will ask him to leave and he will leave. This place will splinter in his mind. A shoe in water. Fingers of light through the leaves. Edward will re-member Jack in his vanishing points. His ankles, his wrists, his neck. The stretch of skin where his shirt came up if he bent at the hip, the shallow depressions above the belt on either side of the spine. Pale places that mosquitoes like.

Snake through time further and find Edward the father in a family. His wife in the living room with the children, the television on, removing lice from their hair, crumpling a tissue over their white pearl eggs and sliding them off the comb. He comes in with his coat on, and she folds her body round him, all care and bones, the children round their ankles like dogs.

Further in the future, find him old. A grandfather. Place a baby in the crook of his arm and a word in his mouth — *Joseph*.

Edward breathed in.

Eleanor

1967

Eleanor kneels with a comb in her hand, her shins pressing into the carpet. Her fingers travel nimbly over her children's scalps, and she counts each louse that she captures. She is thirty-nine years old. For a moment, Eleanor feels the strangeness of life having led her to this pale green living room. She rests her hand upon her daughter's shoulder. Ruth turns expectantly, but Eleanor doesn't speak. What can be said about the peculiar lightness of having arrived in one life rather than another? Then Edward enters and she goes to him.

Emily

1989

I was born two years and seven months after you. Robust and at the proper time, I screamed immediately at the shock of the world: a relief after your crumpled silence. My skin was ready for me, and there had only been a usual amount of pain. Our grandparents brought you to the hospital, where you were allowed to sit on the bed with Mum and hold me, your body leaning against hers, her arm braced round yours.

There is a photograph of this, taken by Grandad so that Dad, standing by the bed, has his head chopped off. Mum looks out at the camera, but you look at me. Babies just born can only see twenty to thirty centimetres in front of them.

Joe, in that moment, you would have been my entire world.

Part One

Joe & Emily

2011

You came home thin at Christmas. The suddenness of it made us laugh, your neck long and pale, and your shoulders not filling your coat. Had you been a young woman, Mum and I might have taken in your sharp collarbones and wrists and exchanged a look. We'd have found a quiet moment to discuss it, quickly changing the subject if you entered the room. I'd have taken you off for a walk on our own, inventing a reason to go to the newsagent's and asking you to come. As we came back together through the quiet streets, I'd have casually asked if you were all right, whether your course was very stressful, touching your arm to show I wanted a real answer. And through my worry and my attempts to buoy you and coax you to me with compliments, I might have felt a little stab of jealousy. Might have grabbed a handful of my own body in bed as you slept in the next room and wondered why I lacked your will.

But you were a man, my brother, always thin and now thinner. I remembered you blowing out your stomach when you were nine years old, the pregnant globe of it funny on your skinny frame. At twenty-four, you hadn't strayed far from that boy-body. You were just taller and more firmly held together, a fine layer of adult muscle over your torso, down the backs of your arms. You seemed happy and confident, four months into your master's. You talked about the music you had been writing and your new friends and your job on Friday and Saturday nights collecting glasses in a cocktail bar. No, you shrugged, you didn't mind giving up those social hours to clear up after other people's fun.

'Too busy to eat,' Dad said.

I poked your ribs as you reached into the kitchen cupboard to move aside mugs in search of your favourite one. You pretended to ignore me as you withdrew it and placed it on the counter. I picked up your forearm. You gave me an impatient look but let it dangle, obligingly limp in my grip.

'God, Joe,' I said, 'you're going to snap.'

Someone had given my boyfriend, Solomon, a packet of cigars and we agreed to try them, laughing at the stranger as Solomon led us into the garden, holding them aloft in his hand: 'Who gives cigars for Secret Santa?'

Dad followed us out with his camera and a beer, and you scowled and asked if he was going to photograph everything that Christmas.

'It's like living with the paparazzi,' you said.

But you still turned toward him as he put his bottle on the wall and waved to get the security light on.

In the image, we are floodlit, with smoke drifting up in front of our faces. I have instinctively slipped into the middle, my arm round Solomon's waist and you narrow at my other side. Your eyebrows are slightly lifted, amusement at the corners of your mouth. We are the adult children, indulging our dad. You look like a gangster in your long black coat, the cigar between your fingers. We are allowed to smoke cigars because they are theatrical somehow and it is Christmas.

You and I were the kind of non-smokers who might say, *Go on then*, a few times a year at parties, holding our gifted cigarettes gingerly and really feeling the nicotine's sick-delicious thump. The rule between us, unspoken, was to never, ever smoke in front of our parents. Solomon could take out a yellow packet at the kitchen table, lay the filter on the paper and sprinkle on tobacco, roll without looking down, lick it and slip out into the garden without comment. Because he was loved less.

On Christmas morning, you opened your presents carefully, using your thumbnail to get under the tape, adding each translucent piece to a ball as you peeled it off. I had learned as a child to pause between presents, so that you wouldn't be left with lots to unwrap after I had finished. We sat on the living-room floor, with Solomon behind us on the sofa. He thanked Mum for every individual gift – socks, shower gel, bottles of beer from around the world, five for ten pounds – touched and self-conscious to be included.

When our parents had moved from the countryside back to London, I was eighteen and you were twenty. New adults. It might have been the moment to stop doing Christmas stockings. But four Christmases had passed since then and here we were. Now, I imagined us in our forties, crouched on the carpet amid sheets of bright paper. We opened cards from our grandad, which depicted choristers with their mouths open in song and contained ten-pound notes. A faint ink mark had transferred onto mine – a broken *H* across the Queen's nose – from his neat, sloping *Happy Christmas*.

After lunch, we folded chocolate wrappers into shining triangles and watched films we had seen before on a projector borrowed from Dad's work. The bottom of the shots spilled over the wall onto the mantlepiece, feet and chins warping over the curve of the wood. Mum kept leaving the room to return with food.

'Eat, Joe,' she urged you. 'Everyone eat!'

Eventually, you shook your head at the dates and oranges, walnuts and circles of waxed cheese, and jerked your hands in a wordless irritated gesture. Then you rose and gathered everything quickly, plates and packets piled into your arms, and returned it all to the kitchen.

Solomon got quietly drunk all afternoon, pissed off, I guessed, at spending Christmas with vegetarians. He disappeared upstairs soon after it got dark and I found him, face down, snoring on the bed with his shoes on.

'Honey,' he said, waking briefly as I undid his laces.

By the time I came back down, Mum and Dad were making their way to bed. We crossed on the stairs. The television was off and the house suddenly quiet. I watched you for a moment from the doorway of the living room. You were reading, stretched along the sofa on your belly, propped up on your elbows.

'Hey,' I said.

You looked up.

'Hey.'

Slim and symmetrical, something neat among the

wrapping paper and mugs and wine-rusted glasses.

'Joe,' I said, 'you look like a sphinx.'

In the kitchen, I made hot chocolate in the microwave and poured whisky into it. I lit a tangerine-scented candle someone had given to Mum. We sat diagonally across from one another at the kitchen table, my chair angled inwards, my feet on the seat and my knees bent up in front of me, your back against the wall and legs stretched over the chair next to you, like someone sitting up in bed. Above us, the sound of the radio, classical music, an occasional murmuring voice, leaked through our parents' bedroom floor.

'That candle stinks like ass,' you said.

I blew it out and switched on the fairy lights Mum had laced across the window. You added the strip lights under the cabinets. I hadn't seen you since October, when you came down on the coach for my birthday with a tin brooch for me in your pocket, protected by a carefully folded paper bag. We messaged each other often, but usually with photographs, not words. The whole pizza that had appeared on the pavement outside your halls of residence had been the subject of an entire series. Now, with your elbows on the table and your chin resting on your knuckles, you said, 'Have you heard about Ryan Worrall?'

'Yes!' I said. 'But tell me everything you know,' feeling only a little guilty at how entertaining it was to share the story of this boy, now man, from our home town, who had been given a suspended sentence for running along Corbar Road one night, smashing car windows with a cricket bat.

We talked about him and other people we had in common: mutual friends and schoolmates we no longer saw, who had come out and who was pregnant again at twenty-four. We dissolved After Eights in our mouths, our eyes on each other, squirming against the reflex to chew, and it felt like one of the late afternoons we had shared in childhood once we were old enough to let ourselves in after school with a key kept in a plastic rock by the back door. We would take off our school ties and watch *Come Dine With Me* on the black-and-white television in the corner of the kitchen, and the house would belong to us for a bit before our parents got back from work.

Sitting at the table transplanted from that home, with its white halo burns and scars on the legs where the dog had chewed it, I at last asked about you. It was two in the morning and we had exhausted everybody else. You smiled, slightly wry, then looked a little cut and glanced at the window. It was dark outside, not the dark we had grown up with, thickly silent at night, the moor swaddling the town, but the diluted fox-dark of South London. There were no buses lurching through the streets because it was Christmas, but occasional cars or footsteps came past, reminding us that there were more streets beyond this one, more and more beyond those. You kept your eyes on the window and said you liked someone. He was another student and you were friends, but you hadn't told him, and he had gone home.

'Will you tell him in January?' I asked, but you said no, he had gone back to Boston; he had only been there for a term.

'Aeroplanes exist, Joe.'

'Yeah.'

You smiled but didn't look convinced.

'His family are pretty religious, so . . .'

You stopped and laughed at yourself and said, 'I always do this. I always never tell them.'

'*Always never* sounds hard,' I said.

'I'm such a twat,' you said.

Then Solomon came downstairs and took a beer out of the fridge and the three of us laughed together about something I don't remember now.

On 27 December, we took the train together to Victoria and said goodbye on the concourse. You walked off toward the coach station with your violin under your arm. Could I have looked back and noticed something in the way you walked? In how you held your back perhaps? You swerved round some people handing out samples of toothpaste and disappeared through the side exit.

As we went down to the Tube, Solomon asked what you were going to do in Birmingham in the weeks before the start of term.

'He'll practise, write music, concentrate,' I shrugged.

The two of you mystified each other but found ways to be, watching documentaries about the Second World War together on Mum and Dad's sofa, eating Hula Hoops off the ends of your fingers.

I told you once that I thought I would marry Solomon and you smiled and said, 'Oh, how nice,' and then we'd talked about something else.

I returned to my flat and did not think about you. You spent New Year's Eve at one of your teacher's houses in Birmingham, and I spent it in Brixton with Solomon and a few hundred strangers, sweating and dancing in the dark and getting tired hours before he was ready to go home. I did not think about your thin wrists, your new brittleness, tension glowing out from some unseen place.

2012

In January, Solomon and I boarded a plane to Belfast. He drank a beer at Gatwick and two more on the hour-long flight, but said he wasn't nervous. We arrived at the little airport in the dark, and his eyes darted around as we walked out, landing on a skinny man in his forties who looked like Solomon's older brother. The man hugged Solomon a little harder than Solomon hugged back. Then he drew away and held his shoulders for a moment, before turning to embrace me, clumsy and excited, like he couldn't believe we were there.

As the three of us went out to his car, he spoke quickly: 'I'm so happy you're here, Sol. So happy! It's just along here. Fuck me, the parking was a rip-off!'

I tried to imagine his accent in Solomon's mouth, the way my boyfriend would have spoken if he'd stayed and grown up here and all the ingredients of his life had been different.

I had only just met Solomon when Sean came back into his orbit. One night in his tiny bedroom, he tensed and told me, 'So, my dad got in touch.'

It was our first real conversation in a way, both of us

forgetting to be gorgeous and fun and non-committal. I lay on my side and listened as he talked, his voice steady and his eyes on the ceiling. He said he wasn't sure whether to reply. Sean used to come back to visit when Solomon and his brother were small, taking them out for the day. He never had any money, so they did things like paddling in the fountains in Trafalgar Square until someone told them off. I pictured the two boys shivering on the bus afterwards in soaking clothes. Eventually, the visits stopped. It struck me as strange for family to be so malleable, its dimensions shifting as people chose to exit and enter. There had been nothing for seventeen years until a message landed in Solomon's phone with a hollow chime. He didn't reply immediately but reread it and reread it and kept clicking *View profile*.

'He looks like me,' Solomon said. 'It's weird. He just looks so much like me.'

I kissed his face really gently, like we knew each other better than we did, and asked what he wanted to do.

Two years on, after exchanging messages, talking twice on Skype and meeting once face to face in London, when they had gone to Brick Lane together and Solomon had come home so drunk that he had risen in the night to piss in the corner of our bedroom, Sean had invited us out to Derry to see him. They had discovered things in common. Small things that felt seismic after so long apart. Solomon's eyes glowed as he told me they both felt strongly that Sister Rosetta Tharpe was the un-hailed queen of rock and roll.

But he had hesitated about the trip. 'Mum won't like it.'

Then Sean offered to pay for the flights, which mattered somehow, though they weren't expensive.

As we drove through the night from Belfast to Derry, Sean asked Solomon to take the wheel for a moment and brought out a tin of tobacco to roll a cigarette on his thigh. Solomon leaned into his space and took a corner as his father talked rapidly, calling him Sol, which no one ever called him. He showed us the sign to the city. Someone had spray-painted *LONDON* out of the name.

All week Solomon was paraded around.

Sean beamed as he said, 'This is my son,' the phrase as full and fresh as if Solomon had just been born.

We went to pubs and met what felt like hundreds of smiling friends, who shook Solomon's hand and looked from him to Sean and back again as if their likeness were some sort of miracle.

'You're short like a Derry girl,' the women told me as I tried to hang back.

The streets were full of shops selling plastic Virgin Marys, and when the pubs closed, people piled back to Sean's house, which was big but freezing with hardly any furniture. Cocaine was lined up on a world atlas. Ketamine. Other things.

'Don't you want any, Emily?' Sean asked, like he was passing round a plate of biscuits.

I had a sad feeling as everyone around me burned through energy into listlessness.

Solomon said, 'It's cool that I can party with my dad,' and chewed his lip.

At ten in the morning, he joined me in bed, took my

hand and said, 'Emily, can you just tell me one thing? Just one thing.'

His hand was damp and chilly. He looked worried.

'What is it, honey?' I asked.

'Are there, like, a hundred spiders crawling out that crack in the ceiling?'

I told him there wasn't even a crack in the ceiling.

On the final night, we ate in a massive, empty Chinese restaurant. Red lanterns and roses on the carpet. A Snoopy figurine in the fish tank. For some reason, a dance floor.

'This is my son!' Sean said to the waitress, a short woman with pale stripes of iridescent highlighter running from her temples to her cheeks.

'Hi,' I said, thinking they knew each other.

But she just said, 'Table for three, yes?' and showed us to a round, glass-topped table set for six, grabbing up the three spare plates, the cutlery and the glasses.

Then she said, 'Wait,' and vanished somewhere.

We all looked at each other, ironic-expectant; then music came on through a speaker above our heads. Synths layered over with flute, a keyboard pretending to be strings. I was about to say my brother had a perverse fascination with this kind of music, tell them that you liked to dissect each layer of its ugliness, but I realised that might sound rude. Sean ordered far too much food. We weren't hungry enough and it sat cooling around us, shining and hardening, decorated with carrots cut like flowers. Together, we made it through one of the three huge plates of egg fried rice as Sean spoke about the video evidence that 9/11 was a hoax.

'If you look at the footage of the second tower—'

My wine glass dropped from my hand, spilling in a streak over the table and onto his shirt.

'. . . you'll see the *way* it collapses,' he continued, dabbing the mark as Solomon handed him napkins, 'just *cannot* be from a plane impact.'

Solomon caught my eye and sucked sweet-and-sour sauce from his fingers.

We said almost nothing as Sean ordered more wine and three banana fritters, swerving somehow onto the topic of Solomon's mum. 'I would *never* hit a woman. The trouble with that situation was her parents. Don't you want that?'

'I don't really like bananas.'

'Sol, you should have said.'

He tried to order shots, but Solomon put his hand out, leaving a faint sticky mark on his father's sleeve.

'Early start tomorrow,' he said.

'I'm driving you to the airport, Sol. You can sleep in the car.'

There was a crackle of tension between the two men when Solomon tried to pay.

'Please,' Sean said, 'for all the time when I wasn't . . . when I couldn't be there to pay.'

Solomon told him, 'Do what you want,' when he was supposed to just say, *Thank you.*

'You OK?' I asked him as we got in bed, but he didn't really answer, just said he was looking forward to going home. He woke me up in the bleary early hours, pulling me toward him. We packed our stuff to leave.

'Shall we wake your dad?' I asked as we went into the hall, the sky still dark outside.

Solomon glanced at the closed bedroom door.

'Sol, shall we wake him up? A cab will cost more than the flights.'

He said, 'Don't you start calling me Sol too,' and gently drummed his knuckles on the door.

We walked out to the plane with the sky turning pink as the sun rose. The lights along the wings glowed pink too. Sometimes the world is so beautiful by accident.

'Well done,' I told Solomon as we took our seats, but he just said, 'For what?'

He didn't drink any beers on the way back.

We touched down with a fanfare and a recorded voice told us we had arrived on *Yet another on-time flight!* I turned my phone on as we waited for the doors to open and it vibrated with a message from Dad.

'That's weird,' I said. 'Mum and Dad have come to meet us.'

'But we're going back to ours,' he said.

'Yeah,' I reassured him, 'we're going back to ours. I don't know why they're here.'

He looked away from me, and I added, 'Don't they have anything better to do?'

As we came out into the car park, they drove past but didn't see us. If there was worry on their faces, I didn't notice. I wanted to show Dad my photographs and to find some time alone with Mum to talk about how strange and slightly sad the trip had been. I'd probably leave out the part about the drugs. I phoned Mum and she said to come up a floor. As we climbed the stairs, they came down. They hugged us in the stairwell.

'What's going on?' I asked, as we followed them up and over the concrete.

Mum held on to my sleeve. Not my arm but my sleeve. I twitched to make her let go. Solomon shrank – a subtle movement, but I saw it, his instinct to be less there.

Dad said, 'We need to tell you something before we get into the car.'

What was wrong with the car? Would we need to get in carefully, or both go in through the same door because the other was broken? When we were children, my best friend, Harriet, had been going along in a car when the door next to her fell off into the road. I had been jealous at the time that something exciting had happened to her instead of me.

Dad said, 'Joe has cancer.'

It did not begin in the airport car park as I tried to absorb the fact. It did not begin two days before, when Mum and Dad came and met you at the hospital in Birmingham and the oncologist came in and said the word *cancer* for the first time. The word did not start it. It did not begin the day before that, when you were there on your own and the oncologist had only said *tumour*, or on the night between those two days as you sat awake on the ward, rough, cold cotton of a hospital gown, working out what *tumour* meant. A student nurse, around your age, had come and sat on the chair by your bed. He chatted to you as you cried. Craig, you told me later – you were almost sure his name was Craig. Craig probably asked what composing music was like, how someone got into that. Or maybe the two of you just spoke about the city and whether he ever came into the bar where you worked. But it did not begin with Craig. It did not begin when you went to your GP with stomach pain, and she felt your stomach with that terrible firm touch doctors have and phoned ahead to the hospital to say that you needed immediate tests. You sat on the bus praying that it wasn't appendicitis because you had so much work to do. Deadlines. It did not begin before that, when the stomach pains were mild, tolerable, and you pressed your palms over your lower belly and held them there, like we press our fingers into our temples to stem a headache, or before that, when the sensations came, sensations that could hardly be called pains. It did not begin in September, when you started your course and volunteered for a drug trial, queuing with the other students for a medical screening that pronounced you a healthy subject, though you were later rejected because the trial was oversubscribed and you did not get to receive £250 and play a vital role in the fight against malaria. It wasn't then. It couldn't have started then. The oncologist said that it had probably been growing for years. It could be genetic – travelling dormant through the bodies of our parents, through the bodies of our mother's parents, who took us to the beach as children and showed us creatures in the rockpools, or our father's parents, who died before we were born – moving through generations, waiting to be expressed, at last, in you.

We cannot know the beginning of the story.

And yet I picture the moment when a cell within you trembled and split. I picture you in your childhood bedroom. Derbyshire. The limestone walls of our old house. It is evening. Light on your face from the fish tank. It happens as you sit straight-backed, your socked feet planted evenly on the floor. I picture you on one of the rare mornings you accompanied me to the swimming pool. It happens in the water as the blade of your hand grazes your ear. Perhaps it's like puberty, which has to start at night. I saw a documentary once that said you have to be asleep for that little flip in your body to occur, the signal that hormones are ready to release, everything within you silently bracing for change. Your body knows then that there has been enough childhood and it is time for something else.

I picture you at a concert. It arrives between blinks as you lift your violin.

It was in your bowel and your liver. Possibly your lung.

'A shadow on his lung,' Mum said, her voice almost level but tears on her face.

She reached toward me, but I ducked, sitting down on the kerb. Did she see that? I did not want to be touched.

'Right,' I said. 'Right, right.'

Dad was passing me a paper cup. They had bought coffee as they waited for me and Solomon, had wanted to get one for each of us, but the first was so massive they had decided we could share.

Joe has cancer.

A silver treble-clef brooch on Mum's cardigan. Cars coming and going. Coins into the machine. Everything metal. Aeroplanes leaving for other places and I could have turned round and got on one of them and missed your last almost-year, skeleton trees into summer and the world bringing out its best, my ears suddenly awake to the heartbeats of mice and the vibration of seeds beneath the ground, going with you for chemo and laughing with you on the ward until the pain swelled your arm too much to slide your sleeve over it and I had to drape your coat across your back. I could have missed it all. Your hands on the sheets like birds. Blueberries spilling across the floor like the sloes found in the stomach of a mummified Chalcolithic man.

Joe has cancer.

I had landed in the wrong country. A close country, but one I did not know. I got in the car.

Solomon took the train and returned to our flat alone, and I travelled up the motorway to you. Sitting in the back of the car was like being on my own. Warm, stale air blew in from the little plastic vents, and Mum and Dad told me, *It is serious . . . We aren't sure how serious yet . . . It's treatable . . . He's just been diagnosed . . . We haven't told anyone else yet . . .* until I closed my eyes and pretended to sleep.

Eventually, Mum leaned between the seats and said softly, 'We're here, Emily,' and I opened my eyes to read, *Welcome to Paradise Circus Car Park.*

We found you outside the City Gardens, standing on the pavement reading a paperback. I expected you to look different, but you looked the same, with your dark hair thick and flicking out at the back where it met your neck. A little tension in your jaw. Tape round one arm of your glasses. Your long coat was open, with a blue hoodie underneath, the zip slightly undone. Glimpse of a stripy T-shirt.

You glanced up and smiled as we approached. You slid a train ticket from the back of the book to mark your place as you closed it.

'For fuck's sake, Joe,' I said as I hugged you.

You shook your head, said, 'I know, right,' and rolled your eyes.

Joking felt wonderful, like we were still smoking cigars in the garden, playing at something we didn't normally do.

We walked through the cold park and then to a café that you liked, where the barista knew you and asked if we were your family. 'Yes,' we all told her across the counter, and she grinned, delighted to be right. One of her teeth stood forward from the rest. She said she wasn't really meant to do this as she printed all of our drinks, four little black ink coffee cups, onto your loyalty card.

I had visited you everywhere you had lived, camped on the floors of your small bedrooms and discovered how fitfully you slept, layered up my clothes in freezing student flats, walked with you through museums and botanical gardens, been introduced – *This is my sister* – and seen gazes travel between our faces, been told that yes, people could see the likeness. The last time I came to Birmingham, we ate digestive biscuits in your shared kitchen and they tasted of bananas because you kept all your food in the same cupboard.

Today felt almost the same, except I was there with Mum and Dad and there were new words. *Oncology. Metastasis.* I didn't ask what they meant. I gathered that cancer had sprouted in your bowel and little spores of it had travelled through you to other parts, where they had settled and begun to grow. None of them were easy parts to remove, like testicles or breasts, and so the cancer would need to be shrunk in place.

'Will you have radiotherapy?' I asked.

'No, the other one.'

Down the line, Dad said, there could then be surgery to trim out what remained.

'I don't know how to tell people,' you said. 'I mean, I don't mind telling them, but they might mind being told.'

'They can get over it,' I said.

Mum sat opposite you. I thought of the exercise where you pretend to sit on an invisible chair to strengthen your thighs. She was perched so lightly. But she smiled. She had put on lip salve with a tint of berry colour in it. She kept touching you.

She laughed when you said, 'My new year's resolution is more chemo.'

A light rain was falling when we got up to leave and Mum urged you to do your coat all the way up. Surprisingly, you complied. You led us, one hand still fastening your top button as the other pushed the door.

Solomon met me at Stoke Newington Station when I came home. He picked my hand up, nervous, his grip a bit limp.

I repeated what I had been told. 'The bowel, the liver, a shadow on the lung.'

'A shadow?'

'I don't know what it means.'

It was dark. Ahead of us, a shape slipped between parked cars as we turned into our road.

'Do you see the fox?' I said, dropping his hand to point. He squinted for a moment, but it was gone. I told him that you'd be starting treatment next week.

'That's quick,' Solomon said.

'Yeah,' I said. 'It's good, isn't it?'

My voice stretching a little thin, I slowly recounted some more facts of it. I told him you were in good spirits.

'Stage four?' he said. 'How many stages are there?'

He had made huge plates of pasta, which felt solid in my throat no matter how much I chewed.

That night when he was asleep, I sat with my back against the door in the bathroom with my laptop on my legs. I searched for survival rates. There was a crack in the sink. I read for a long time, until the battery was hot against my thighs. Then I closed down all the windows and never thought about those numbers again.

I emailed Harriet. The friend I had made aged five, when I reached out and picked up the orange tassel of hair at the end of her plait. It was resting on the classroom carpet, where we sat cross-legged learning about the life cycle of frogs. Harriet's home was the first place I ever stayed overnight without a blood relation.

Hey, Harri, my email began. The subject line was *Difficult News*.

I had shared her with you. Automatically. Though you were older than me, I often did things first. I sat on the step to tie my own laces – *Ears of the rabbit, round the tree, into the rabbit hole* – and made friends, before you had worked out how to do either. But you were always much better at answering questions like *What weighs more, a tonne of lead or a tonne of feathers?* You were shy, I was told, but it just seemed to me like my place in the world was running forward through the park squealing, my fingers interwoven with Harriet's and my teeth chomping painfully through my tongue when one of us tripped and both fell to the ground, and yours was with Mum or Dad on the path, slipping your body half behind theirs if someone you did not know stopped to speak to them. *Look at this, Joe!* I would yell, running to you with a felled daffodil. You would point out the veins in the papery sheath round the flower, how like an onion it was. *Look at this, Joe!* Harriet would cry, running to you with a rock.

One morning, when the three of us were all in primary school, there was so much snow that only half the children and two of the teachers made it in. We were herded into the hall, where we sang carols all morning instead of having lessons. The snow muffled the world outside and your teacher asked you to go to the front and play the violin. Harriet beamed at me, as if you belonged to both of us, in the slip of stillness before your bow landed on the strings. When a girl behind ruined it by whispering, *That's Emily's weird brother*, it was Harriet who got sent into the corridor to reflect on how it was not nice to kick. She never got in trouble. It was so incongruous to see her as we filed out, her pale, placid face staring at the wall.

She came out to see me when I left home to work in Austria. I was eighteen and homesick and a little shocked by the reality of young children – my main job as an au pair seemed to be scrubbing diarrhoea out of Disney-princess knickers. We passed through mountains on the train to Vienna. The snow blasted light into the carriage. Harriet asked if I knew that you were gay. The two of you had gone for a drink and you had told her. *Yes*, I said, though you and I had not discussed it. It was like being told your hair colour, taking a second to call your face to mind, then agreeing, *yes*, that is right.

Now she was the one living elsewhere. You and I joked that she was *somewhere building orphanages*, though she was actually studying in Canada.

Her reply to my email came swiftly. *Dear Emily*, it began, *I love you (both /all) so much.*

Term started. I trudged to the Regent's Park campus and cried in a basement room with a man I didn't know. There were plants on his desk, ferns and other things that didn't need too much light. He nodded and signed a pink form requesting that my essay deadlines be extended.

'You can come back, you know,' he said. 'We could start a regular session to talk this through.'

'No, thank you,' I said, swinging my bag onto my shoulder. 'Thanks for the mitigating circumstances.'

In class, I sat by the cool of the windows, quieter than I had been before, rarely raising my hand. Mid-January, cold and metallic, like something surgical withdrawn from a packet by a skilled gloved hand. Talk about language, about the way plots are stitched together, narrative modes. Analyse this passage. Free indirect discourse. I felt empty. Naturalism versus the modernists.

'Now, this is exciting stuff!' the lecturer said. How memory occurs to us. Voluntary memory. Involuntary memory. Narrative voice enacting it, opening the door.

You put your fist through a door once. The glass door between the kitchen and the front porch. You were seventeen and about to audition for college, nervous, agitated all the time. Something sparked in you and you threw your fist at it. There were hairs in the doorframe where the dog had slid past just after the wood was painted. *Joe!* Mum shouted. But she also stepped forward, placed her hand in the centre of your back and said, *It's all right. Just don't move.* Your naked feet surrounded by glass. *High pain threshold*, Mum had said. Blood on your knuckles and glass at your feet, you sort of smiled and muttered, *Oh fuck*, almost as if it had calmed you down.

There was a small commotion at the front as the lecturer pulled the screen down from the ceiling and struggled to focus the projector. A few people shouted suggestions and the rest grew impatient, striking up murmured conversations. I turned my whole body to the window. Below the classroom, a man carried a dachshund down the street, his elbow bent, the dog's long belly draped over his arm. The dog sailed serenely above the man's quick strides.

If something terrible happens, I told myself, the voice inside my head very clear and adult, *I shall get a puppy*. I wanted to laugh, but the lecturer had resumed his presentation. I didn't want anyone to look at me or to ask what I was laughing at. My phone made a shape on my leg through my trouser pocket. I wanted to text you – *If you die, I'll get a dog and call it Joe*. It was just your sort of humour, except your death was in the middle of it.

Months later, our great-aunt would say, *And when's the funeral?* on the phone, when she meant, *And when is the operation?* You would have found it hilarious, if only I could have told you.

In the canteen, I sat quiet opposite my friends. Everyone was eating red things. Yusuf squirted ketchup onto his pizza slice. Claire told him that was disgusting. She lifted her spoon and a spot of tomato soup fell onto her pale jacket.

'Now who's disgusting!' he said.

She ignored him and asked, 'Are you all right, Emily?'

I blinked at her and tried to smile, feeling the movement of my lips lift the muscles in my face. I had always felt old around them. Unlike you, I had faltered after school, working in a pub – an ache in my arm at the end of a shift, my shoes sticking to the floor, being flirted with across half a metre of wood – and then a series of provisional jobs. Three gap years. Now I was twenty-two and these friends, leaning slightly toward me across the melamine table, were nineteen. Yusuf, a drummer, beat his fingers reflexively against his thigh. I lived with Solomon, and these two lived in halls of residence and were still learning how to go to the supermarket and come out with things that would sustain them. I should not have spoken about you.

I told them and there was a beat of silence, then the questions – *What kind? What stage? How old is he?*

Then Yusuf said, 'I'm sure he will be all right.'

Claire said, 'My grandma died of that.'

And then the subject was closed.

I began to arrive just as classes started and to leave quickly afterwards. I put on my headphones and turned the volume up until my ears felt sick. The music helped me to feel like I was just dreaming about being there. I had worked as a tour guide the previous summer, stood on the top deck of an open-top bus with a microphone in a white shirt and a red clip-on tie, pointing out interesting places and sometimes making up dates rather than answering, *I don't know*, to people's questions. You came down to London one Saturday and sat on my bus beside an old French woman. We caught eyes and smirked when she thanked you for being her date before she got off at the Victoria Embankment, her ancient hand gripping the railing all the way down the stairs.

Now, I found myself sorting through the facts – small, safe objects I could reach into my pockets for. *Nelson's Column is 169 feet tall. St Martin-in-the-Fields was built in 1721. It was the model for the town hall in* Back to the Future. Joe has cancer. *Pigeon shit corrodes Portland stone.*

During this time, the initial weeks after diagnosis, there were many things I was not involved with. You sat in waiting rooms in Birmingham with sheet music in your lap, frowning over a page, a pencil in your hand. Mum and Dad poured coffee into a thermos flask and travelled up the motorway to sit beside you at each consultation. You scheduled appointments around lectures, attempted normality. You thought you could fold it into your life. Chemotherapy would come in rounds and there were long discussions about what you could do when in order to remain on your course. You quickly banned Mum from consultations because you couldn't stand her questions, the way she would blurt out – *And what about the rest of us? Can we give any organs? I've heard turmeric is good. Is turmeric any good?* – looking guilty as soon as she'd spoken, like a child who has reached for something she knows she's not allowed, small, wide-eyed, unable to help herself. After this, she guarded your things in the waiting room and you went in with Dad.

What was supposed to happen?

This beginning stage is hard to recall. This slip of time as January became February and you were prodded and tested and a plan was conceived. You would begin chemotherapy on 9 February. If it worked, an operation would follow. Your blood was taken, again and again, little labelled vials clinking on a table in front of a nurse. You would need medicines, so many that Dad had to make a spreadsheet of when you were supposed to take them. And you were scanned. I never saw the machine, but I picture something between a photocopier and an X-ray, you lying still on a white shelf, a blade of light travelling from your head to your toes.

Our parents always called me as they travelled back from your appointments. Mum's voice taut between reassurance and fear. Dad beside her at the wheel, his eyes on the road, interrupting with corrections. *No, Ruth, that's not what they said.* But the contours of what they told me have vanished. Perhaps I never really listened at all.

On the first Saturday of February, I went to Victoria and climbed onto a coach in thin, rain-soaked shoes. You would begin chemo the following Tuesday. It was not the sort, apparently, that would make you lose your hair. A man with acne-scarred cheeks sat beside me and spoke incessantly for the whole journey. He tore open a packet of peanuts and crunched them noisily, salt sticking to his lips, told me all about the conference he was going to and asked me questions – *What's your name? What kind of music do you like? Do you want some peanuts? Have you been watching* Wonders of the Universe? I didn't know how to make him not do that and wanted to shout, *I don't care, I don't care.*

'What a prick,' you said, when I told you about him.

I opened a tin of Vaseline and we both dipped our little fingers into it and spread some over our lips. I didn't mention that on the outskirts of the city, the man had asked why I was going to Birmingham and I had told him, stupidly, that I was visiting my brother who had cancer. How he had said, *Cancer is so misunderstood. It's seriously amazing what you can do with natural remedies. There's this drink kombucha, it fixes everything. Seriously, have you heard of kombucha?*

We walked around a bookshop and you picked up *1001 Movies You Must See Before You Die* and said, 'I'd better get a move on.'

I laughed and said, 'Don't ever say that to Mum.'

You took me to Birmingham Symphony Hall to listen to soaring music. The orchestra lifted their instruments and the choristers stood. I kept glancing at you, because I was afraid I would get something wrong, would clap between movements. This was a thing you knew the rules of. You sat alert in your red seat with your hands in your lap. The cellos began alone, in a low whisper, then were joined by the higher instruments. The deep voices threaded in, quietly, gradually, then the higher voices. As soon as everyone was together, the instruments fell away and the voices became very loud and powerful in their sudden nakedness. I noticed tears shimmering in your eyes. I watched the singers all turn their pages together in a soft wave over their black clothes. Tears fell down my face, but when I looked back at you, your tears were gone.

Afterwards, we got on a bus toward the coach station. You wanted to take me, though I could have travelled alone, so I pretended to be too cold to walk, in case you were tired. It was late. A rugby team piled on between us. I boarded first and turned to speak to you, only to find you were stuck behind this swathe of boys. Strong but podgy, not quite formed. Excited by the idea of being men. Bodies full of beer. Liquid faces. A little hesitant. Wanting to take up space. Checking what was allowed.

One was wearing a wound on his elbow, dark, knotted over with blood. 'Shall we do it?' he asked another boy, eager and unsure.

'Yeah, let's just do it,' said the friend. 'Let's do it now!'

The wounded boy lifted his chin and chanted as loud as he dared, 'Arooga ba arooga!' and all the boys replied, 'Arooga ba aroo!' Timid-bold.

I caught your eye and you raised an eyebrow. The whole bus glowed with how much I loved you.

I knew that our bodies could be hurt.

Aged four, I picked up a kitchen knife. The memory is not of the second when my skin broke but the moment after: Mum on the floor beside me, pressing paper towels into my hand. The blood and the way she said, *It's my fault. It's my fault*, as I put my little mouth upon the cut. Once, I leaped off the sofa and landed with my face in the carpet and you leaped off after me and landed on my arm. The moment is gone – the bone snap. But I recall a nurse winding plaster-soaked bandages round my forearm, how they hardened to a cast, which you drew on with felt-tip pens, the particular ache of a bone healing and the sight of my pale, deflated limb the day the cast came off. A blue foxglove grew in the corner of our infant-school playground and a dinner lady stood in front of it every playtime to protect us from its poison.

On holiday with our grandparents, a wasp stung you and your ankle swelled, the skin hot to the touch. I think you were seven. Grandad filled a plastic bowl with cool water and you placed your foot in it. Pink except for the centre of the sting, which was white. You sucked air through your teeth and pushed the heels of your hands into your eyes. Grandad held your shoulder and told you to count to ninety-nine. Afterwards, I put my feet in the bowl, although I didn't need to, and Grandma shook talcum powder onto a towel, which we stepped onto. Then she sprinkled the tops of our feet. It was a lovely feeling. We trod white footprints through the caravan.

You never broke a bone.

I would like to pause here Joe, hold you safe, untouched by treatment. Your body never hurt beyond repair.

Edward

1939–1945

Come back through time and find a small face between lengths of black cloth.

Edward Blood stood in the coat cupboard, grinding tablets of mud from the shoes into dust with his foot. He was four years old. Dexterous enough for scissors but his eyes still a bit big in his skull. Somewhere else, a war was starting as his body disappeared. He clasped his hands together and drew in his shoulders, narrowing himself. Happiness. Beyond this, the house. A pine cross on the landing with a metal Jesus draped over it. Edward opened and closed his eyes in the dark. Then a hand reached in, parted the coats and took his wrist.

His mother kneeled in front of him. She placed her forehead between his ear and his shoulder.

'I couldn't find you,' she said.

Far in the future, Edward would look at photographs and realise how very small this woman was, her eyes widely spaced and anxious, her skin weather-worn and dry.

'Don't rummage in people's pockets,' she said.

As she walked away, Edward kept his eyes on her back.

Curiosity lit up within him. Returning to the cupboard, he turned out the pockets one by one, discovering chicken feed, a few coins and, in his sister's pocket, the head of a doll, popped from its body, with mud in the recesses of its eyes as if Agnes had found it in the road. Examining these treasures became his first clear memory.

Here is Edward's early life.

His rebellions were small and infrequent, performed in silence when everyone was outside or in a different room. Agnes, who was two years older than him, disturbed things, unable to close doors without slamming them, working a nail loose from the fence outside, hiding it in her sleeve, then carving her initial into the wood of her wardrobe. Edward stood mute in the doorway as his mother sanded off the *A* with brisk circles, taking a little of her skin with it and biting her mouth like she might cry.

Edward's quietness emerged, luckily, into a house that favoured it. The sounds of his mother were of work, not speech, the *push, push* of a brush in the yard or the metal bottom of a bucket being set down. Sometimes, a tiny clicking came from her, and the miniscule sounds of her lips moving without voice, beads travelling through her fingers as she uttered silent prayers. His father smiled benignly from the corners of rooms. He was deaf and lip-read and had a way of casting his eyes away from the person speaking in order to close a subject. The pink tip of Edward's tongue often darted between his teeth then re-treated, a silent letter forming before a word would come. He discovered things you can only touch by being very quiet and careful, like the back of a bumblebee, soft as it looked, as it made its way into a flower. He was delighted by the bones of birds, and the delicious feeling of scissor blades gliding through newspaper, the letters from *war* perfect for the centre of his name.

When he was seven, his teacher was a very thin woman called Miss Randall and Edward developed the idea that he would grow up to marry her. She had a discreet layer of golden fur all over her body, which he would learn decades later was a sign of anorexia. To him then, she simply seemed illuminated. He stared at his own face in the mirror as his mother dipped a comb in water before church and drew back his hair, the teeth pleasant against his scalp. The pair of them were both dark with deep-set eyes, but he had his father's large ears. Periodically, she kneeled on the floor beside the bath and trimmed his hair, the black strands falling past his shoulders and floating around his knees. One evening, Edward turned and she nicked his ear, a spot of blood falling onto the enamel and running down in a stripe to the water, like the blood dribbling from Christ's palms. When everyone closed their eyes at church, Edward sometimes allowed his to drift open. Imagine if human beings slept like that, he thought, sitting up together in rows. Beside him, Agnes struggled to be good, her eyelids repeatedly flickering up, repeatedly clamped closed. Then the best part: they would all open their eyes and sing.

One day, when he was nine, the woman who ran the choir took Edward's mother aside as they were leaving via the front steps. He did not know her name, but for a long time had been mesmerised by her ankles. She did not seem to have any. The flesh swelled out at the necks of her shoes into thick trunks that disappeared into her skirt. He wondered if she also had no knees. If her legs were like tubes all the way up. On the way home, his mother said Mrs Galvin had asked if he would like to join the choir. It had been noted that he sang in tune. He had noticed that those around him wobbled and droned, seeming to fall one after the other away from the melody, the way that the boys who stood balancing on the back of a bench in the schoolyard all began to drop off if one lost his footing.

It was an unquestioned fact that his mother only left the farm on Sundays, and so the following week, Edward sat with his father on Mrs Galvin's couch. There was a piano against one wall, with a framed photograph on top of it of a young man in uniform with a sparse moustache. His father's body and hands seemed obscenely large in the small room. Edward stood in the middle of the rug and sang, while Mrs Galvin played, her feet making a *put, put* sound on the piano's peddles. His voice rose clearly from his body. *Soul of my Saviour, sanctify my breast; body of Christ, be thou my saving guest.* Mrs Galvin twisted round on her stool and beamed at him, and his father, who nodded and smiled as if he had also heard.

Edward was surprised by how exciting it was to have been chosen for something, to stand with the choir, separate from the rest, adults and children, their voices mixing, harmony forming in the spaces between each part. It was like a place, the part of himself that understood the music, a realm where the notes lived. Shiny things with clean edges.

The war ended. Frank, a young man with a lisp who had

helped at the farm sometimes, had been killed in a place called Rangoon. He had once crouched beside Edward to tell him that quiet bulls are the most dangerous because it was easy to forget their strength, each *s* escaping as *th* from his lips. Mr Williams had also died, and the neighbours' sons, Samuel and John. For a while, a few children in Edward's class had excitedly brought out letters, unfolding and refolding them until the pieces came apart in their hands. He had felt slightly jealous. But the letters were soon put away. As an adult, Edward would wonder if all this ordinary death had inured him somehow. Later still, he would find it had not.

He stood shyly with Agnes among a lot of people in the paddock behind a pub. Victory. Someone handed him a glass of lemonade, damp on the outside so it slipped through his grip. There was a blue balloon tethered to a table of cakes. Their parents were not there, and today he noticed it, their strange reluctance to leave home. The thought landed clearly because everyone else was there – the population of his life. Twice Edward was found in the crowd. First it was to sing 'Poor Old Michael Finnegan' with the schoolchildren. They must have also sung something else, but what he would remember was shouting, *Begin again!* as the adults chatted and half listened. Seeing one of their neighbours, beaming, radiantly drunk, placing his hand upon his wife's buttock. Then Edward sang with the people from church, sending a different feeling through the crowd. *Be still, my soul, the Lord is on thy side.* A streak of something sad and serious through the joy.

'Oh, Edward!' Mrs Galvin said afterwards.

Her son had survived. There were tiny purple veins in her cheeks. She threw her arms around him. Scent of beer and dried roses.

'You have magnificent lungs!'

1946

Suddenly, one term, Edward found himself cut off at school. No one wanted to play with him or sit by him. They shot him guilty glances and whispered behind their hands. When he tried to approach, they ran away screeching, gleeful, pretending to be afraid. A few years before, a timid evacuee had sat at the front of the class and a silvery louse had been noticed, crawling out of his collar and up his neck. Edward had felt for the shunned child – if only he had sat at the back. But at least that boy had known his crime. Each break time, as Edward walked in circles round the yard – less humiliating than standing alone – he tried to work out what he had done.

And then in assembly, the new boy, Jack, leaned close to him and whispered, 'People say your house is haunted.' His eyes round, thrilled.

They were standing next to each other, Edward's left shirt sleeve touching Jack's right, sheet music in their hands. The children started singing and there was no time to ask questions. Edward felt strange, like he was looking at the group of them from the outside, lined up, opening and closing their mouths like fledgling birds.

That evening, as usual, he followed his mother out to the chicken coop. It was cool and still. The seed felt dry through his fingers as it ran to the ground. The chickens gathered close to him, the white ones, the two tawny ones and the single black one – his favourite. His mother slid her hands into their straw and pulled out eggs. There was a bramble scratch on her forearm, her vulnerable part, always exposed so the hairs were sun-bleached. It was dusk. They never spoke much as they did this, but Edward found himself repeating what he had heard, his eyes on the gloss feathers of the black chicken. Her back was to him. Much later, he would wonder if her face had changed in this moment, whether anything crossed over it before the flat expression she wore when she turned round. He expected her to say something, but she just moved her head slightly, tilted her chin down. She looked at him. Her hair in a tight bun on her head. Whenever Edward saw it unpinned, he was amazed at how much of it there was, dark and crinkled from plaiting, hanging almost to her waist. She didn't speak. There was an egg in her hand.

'Why do they think that?' he said.

'Because people died here.'

'Oh,' he said. Then he asked, 'How many people?'

'Four.'

'Who?'

'My mother, my father, my uncle and my brother,' she said, and put the egg into the box by her feet.

When they went back into the house, Edward thought about it existing for a long time before he was born, belonging to people he did not know. A whole family that his mother was part of, but he and his father and sister were not.

The next day, he asked Agnes about it as they walked down the hill to school. She had been told things, not by their mother but by a woman in church, and more things by a friend of hers, who had been told by her mother, who had been told by the woman who set her hair. Edward had thought of his family as sealed at the top of the hill, and it was strange to discover that other people had been discussing them.

Their mother's family had been carried off one by one by tuberculosis in the wet, early months of 1930 and she had been left suddenly alone on the farm. She was twenty-two. There had been a time afterwards when people were afraid to be near her. Or perhaps she had been afraid of them. She sent away neighbours and stood apart in church.

Edward walked silently next to Agnes. It did not yet occur to him that this period in his mother's life might, must even, have been the beginning of her reluctance to leave the farm. A hare dashed in front of them when they reached the mouth of the lane.

That day, Edward began his solitary walk around the playground, very aware of all of his limbs, his head down but a prickly sensation in his back. He didn't dare glance up to check if he was being looked at. Then the new boy, Jack, was at his elbow. Edward stopped walking and Jack withdrew two pale orange sweets from a paper bag, which was slightly stuck to them.

'You can have this,' he said, passing one to Edward.

He peeled off the residue of paper. He licked the tips of his fingers as he placed the sweet in his mouth. They stood still. Jack rattled his sweet against the back of his teeth and Edward copied him.

Then Jack removed his sweet with his forefinger and thumb, held it to the light and asked, 'Have you ever seen an insect preserved in amber?'

'No,' Edward said.

'They can actually be thousands of years old.'

He said his dad had a paperweight with an ancient fly in it and if Edward wanted to, he could come to his house to look at it. Edward took out his own sweet, smoothed slim so the light shone through it, and held it up like Jack.

'Really?' he said.

Their friendship formed swiftly, with an ease and intensity that neither noticed because they were children. They would lie on their stomachs together with the feather atop its entry in the encyclopaedia, its barbs quivering beneath their breaths as they recited, *Calamus. Rachis. Scapus. Vane.* As they shelled broad beans at the table, Jack's mother talked about stars. *Have you heard, boys, of the Great Dark Horse? The Snake Nebula – shaped like an s? The Little Ghost?*

Edward thought about ghosts. Sometimes at night, he felt frightened of the little boy who had lived there before him: his mother's brother, who had his name first. Sometimes he looked for a milky little face in the white folds of the curtain. Then he got older and the power fell out of it.

1947

The hottest summer Edward had ever lived through. He was twelve years old and had spent a year at the grammar school, standing beside Jack in its bigger, more impressive choir, their young voices slicing through the thicker, lower voices of the older boys. Jack's yellow kite flew above them. Fruit fermented in the trees and the birds all flew home drunk.

There is something to be said for leaving them here, in this summer, before sex. The hedges full of lives. The world fascinating. Touching the stomach of Jack's docile Labrador to guess how many pups were inside. Sometimes letting themselves play like younger children, if no one else was there. Jack grabbing Edward's hand. The way your arm yanks when you don't realise the other person is about to run. Joy and shock of suddenly being in motion over the grass.

Then time carried on.

1949–1952

Edward Blood was fourteen and in charge of the chickens. He held one under his arm, shushing it as he parted its feathers and tweezered out the maggots that had gathered round a wound, their white bodies plump between the blades. He had grown, suddenly, painfully. It was as if his body, already slight, had simply been stretched out. An ache in his bones.

Sometimes, his mind returned to his mother, alone in their house, before Edward or his sister existed. Did she wait to feel ill? he wondered. Did she check her reflection in the hall mirror for signs of sickness, until she realised it wasn't coming? And afterwards, did she still look? Did she meet her own eyes in the glass, as if to say, *You are still here. There is still a person here?*

He was fifteen. His voice broke, cleaving, for a time, into two parts. A nurse appeared at school and slid needles into everyone's arms. The vaccine travelled coolly into him, slightly hardening the place where it had entered. The boys punched each other on their sore arms. He was left with a tiny scar that looked like a burn, as if something hot had struck him but immediately been deflected.

One Saturday, Edward sat with his mother in the parlour behind the kitchen. She picked up a china dog and said, 'My mother's,' quietly. 'There used to be a pair, but I broke the other one with my skipping rope.'

She smiled and a little crack in time opened that let him glimpse her as a girl: Mary Webb, with freckles and teeth a few millimetres too long. Perhaps he could ask her anything and she would answer him flatly, the way she had spoken that evening when he was eleven, the night gathering around them and chickens at their feet.

At some point, Edward Blood began to realise that his best friend was a very beautiful person. It began with stabs of jealousy. Jack seemed so much more carefully made than Edward was. Edward's hair was a dull dark brown. His wrists showed at the end of his sleeves. He hated his neck. He felt slighted by the perfect distance between Jack's head and the ground, between the tips of his shoulders and his collarbones. But the jealousy became something else. He thought about how strange it was that hair was described as a particular colour when actually, every strand on Jack's head had its own colour. Some light brown. Some yellow. Some gold. And his body. Imagine stitching a suit for a person like that, Edward thought. What a joy it would be to write all their measurements in a small book, to translate that body into cloth.

Edward was sixteen. For a month his sister's voice rose jagged in other rooms, his mother's joining it, urgent and hushed. Edward envied his father, who could skulk out of a room and close the door behind him, then hear nothing of what was said. Then Agnes moved away and all the sound seemed to seep from the house.

He discovered the place by accident.

At seventeen, Edward had developed the habit of pausing by the side of the road on his way back from school, gathering the strength to get up the hill to home. The strength to be at home. He would slip off his bike and stand for a while, birds calling and the breeze drying his sweat. If anyone stopped, he would redden – *No, not a flat tyre, thank you. No, not lost, thank you. I'm* – a pause, maybe a bird alighting or returning to a branch – *just waiting.* As the stranger moved off, he would look down and notice the metal shining through where he'd scratched the paint off the crossbar. Flecks of black on his thumbnail.

Then one day it began to rain, sudden and heavy, and he hurried from the verge to the hedge. He stood shivering by it, throwing his bike down so that he could clutch his school bag to his chest. The road darkened as he glanced around for shelter. Then he saw the gap, a few paces ahead of him. On the other side of the hedge was a secret place, hidden and almost dry. It was enclosed by the factory wall on one side, with a stream running beside it, and the wood on the other. The world fell away that afternoon, as Edward stood, listening to the rain. He took a pear from his bag and ate it slowly, letting himself notice the tiny push of resistance before the skin gave beneath his teeth.

Forty-five years later, he would find himself on holiday in Singapore, a scrim of peeling skin on the back of his neck and scalp. The sky would break apart, sending water crashing to the ground. And as he hurried to put away his newspaper, his body would remember how he had once scrambled to a hedge for shelter and found a place that felt empty and safe.

That first night, Edward lay in bed, his damp clothes draped to dry on the chair. The world was fresh and peaceful after the rain. He knew he would go back there. And he did, almost every day. He would slip through the hedge and pull his bike in after him, crouch on a log and read for a while or walk down as far as he could: about thirty yards, before plants blocked the path.

The quiet there was different from the quiet at home. Their farm sat exposed at the top of a hill. It felt stripped quiet. If you shouted there, nothing echoed back: your voice just flowed away from you over the grass. Sometimes a moan rang out, from the gate or a cow, stretching its neck to call to another cow. In the hidden place, there was a thickness to the quiet; everything muffled but alive with tiny noises. Water and birds. Insects. Cars along the road. The machines deep in the factory behind the wall, and the vehicles rolling in and out of its yard. Traces of voice.

Occasionally, a shoe flew over the wall and smacked into the water, making Edward jolt, then relax. This was always followed by a whoop from the factory yard and another voice laughing, scolding his friend, *For God's sake, Sid*. Grown men pretending to be boys for a moment before they went back in from their cigarettes. These invasions angered Edward at first, but he came to like them. They made the place feel truly secret. Those men seemed to think their wall marked the edge of the Earth. And there he stood, beyond it.

He decided to bring Jack there.

That first afternoon, they played a game in which they held their breaths. Jack in front of Edward. That light hair and a mole in his lip. Mesh of hair on his cheeks, visible only in certain kinds of light. The woods and the water quiet but moving. Then Jack breathed out. Then Edward. And then Jack stepped forward and kissed Edward on the mouth. Edward stayed very still – movement would be confirmation or denial. Then he kissed back.

They began to go there, cycling fast, slipping through the hedge and treading down the nettles encroaching on the path – there is a way to flatten them without getting stung if you go slowly and roll the foot from heel to toe. At school they stood, as they had always done, side by side, singing, listening for each other's voices among the choir, knowing that later they would be alone. Once, they peddled so hard to get there that Jack flew from his bike and landed hard on the road, cutting his elbow, and when they were alone, Edward held Jack's arm and licked off the blood. Fresh, disgusting taste of it and a thump of danger. But they were safe there.

They never spoke about it. Language, too, would be confirmation or denial.

Something like this happened before Edward was born. Two people drawing closer without any words. His mother collapsed in church, her body a wrung-out rag from trying to maintain the farm alone. Someone had pulled her up, slid their arms round her from behind and half led, half carried her out, her body cooling rapidly and feeling strangely light. *It's all right, Mary. It's all right. It's all right*, they had said. Glancing back, she saw all the eyes turned upon her. The accusation, as always, was not in their looking but in their looking away. Later that day, the priest had come to her to say he knew a man who could help her, a man looking for a job. He was deaf but hard-working. His name was Thomas Blood.

Thomas slept in the outhouse and then in the house, in the room her brother and uncle had shared. On the first night, she had turned her face down into her mattress, feeling the presence of the almost-stranger through the wall. She gripped the sheets and pushed away the thought that she had allowed this big person to trample through the special emptiness of that room, that she had removed her brother's bed as if he never was. Then one night, she felt a draught passing over her, which was strange as she had slept in that exact spot all her life and never shivered before.

The next day, between tasks, she slipped back into the house and up the stairs and dragged her bed across the room. That night, the wall was cold against Mary's ear. She had, she found, a compulsion to hear his breathing through the wall and something like fear accompanied it; the breaths and little grunting sleeping sounds confirmed for her that Thomas was still alive. But there was another feeling, similar to the rush of energy the night before her birthday as a little child, which she had had to diffuse by kicking her legs under the sheets. Happiness? The anticipation of happiness? Over many nights, the wall, the membrane between them, began to feel thinner, a breakable piece of skin, the solid formation on top of heated milk that Mary had once fished out and given to her brother on a teaspoon, something weak like the flesh of an eyelid. Hard to see at all in the dark.

Gradually, Edward and Jack learned not to flinch at the other's touch. To place a hand on the other's leg, knowing it would be received, that the flesh beneath the palm would not tense. The trick was to contain each touch. To act like any movement – touching the face with the back of the fingers, sliding a hand under the shirt to touch the skin of the back – was just itself, not leading anywhere. Then another movement could be made. Thumb and forefinger undoing buttons. Then the caution could fall away.

But their hidden place broke open. Edward had noticed rubbish in the water sometimes but told himself it must have been hurled over the wall. Like the dud shoes. And then one day, Jack's glance darted away from Edward and he froze. The colour slid out of his lips. Edward turned to see a tramp watching them from across the stream, his hand moving inside his trousers. They ran. They cycled away so quickly Edward thought he might vomit on the grass by the back door when he got home.

When they next saw each other at school, they didn't talk about it. It would be too strange to begin talking now. Jack's expression was closed. Edward couldn't catch his eye. Fear between them. The reinstating of distance. In choir, they did not let their shoulders touch. It began to feel like none of it had happened. Years ago, Agnes had played a game with the chickens, stamping to make them scatter in the yard, then rattling the cup of grain to bring them all back. *Look how stupid they are*, she said, as they scrambled off and returned. Now Edward watched Jack, looked away, looked back. He found himself leaving immediately after choir practice, only to stop abruptly in the street, hoping Jack would catch him up. He never did. Term ended.

Edward was given a record player for his birthday – a miracle really – and it was a reason for Jack to come over. To sit together on Edward's bed, their backs against the white wall, listening to the music. It swelled over all the sounds of the house. Edward's family moving in the other rooms, the animals outside. Edward closed his eyes. The world fell back. Their fingers touched. Edward ran his fingertips over the back of Jack's hand and then up, grazing his arm.

This is what his mother saw: Edward pulling up the fabric of Jack's shirt to put his hand on the pale flesh of his stomach, bringing his lips to his neck, the flash of terror and skin as the two bodies hurriedly pulled apart. Then she closed the door.

Nothing was said that day or that evening as they ate. But the next morning, she came into his room and placed herself on the edge of his bed. There was a loose cotton tip at the side seam of her dress, which she kept touching without looking at it. Her hair, a few grey strands wiry through the black, was pulled so tightly from her face that she seemed to be thrusting forward, her skull somehow closer to her skin than other people's. Rope of plait bound into a bun.

'I think you should go away for a while,' she said.

Edward's face felt hot as she explained, quickly and to her hands, that he had been invited to stay with a friend of his father who lived in France. He had not thought his father had any friends. He was so shy. He sent Edward into the shop to buy his cigarettes rather than going in himself, in case he couldn't lip-read if the man at the counter spoke to him with his back turned as he took them from the shelf.

'What friend?' Edward asked.

'From when he was your age,' she said.

It felt stupid. Untrue. A joke against him, though his parents didn't tell jokes. Edward's father was now fifty-two years old. Did men that age have friends? Edward's face burned.

'What friend?' he said again.

'They write to each other.'

'Mum—' he said.

'You can learn French,' she told the floorboards. Voice soft again. Quiet.

'What for?'

There was a silence in which she looked at him, bruised, then looked away and brought her face back brighter to say, 'Please, Edward.'

And it was the gesture, rather than the words, that made him want to rescue it, to pretend, as she was doing, that she was offering a gift and not a punishment. Her face had such a set quality that any shift in expression was powerful. When he sang in church, he sometimes looked out and saw her nodding slightly in her pew, and it always amazed him to have provoked such a reaction. To see her sharpness relax, to be the cause of that.

Looking at his legs, Edward said it was *a wonderful idea*, the phrase horrible, too full and theatrical in his mouth.

'Wonderful,' she repeated.

She touched his arm, bent at the waist and re-knotted the laces of her boots. Then she stood and went out.

He thought of calling Agnes. Edward pictured going into town, standing inside the phone box and calling. But there was only blank after that. All the small stages seemed insurmountable. Putting the coins in, speaking to the operator. Saying hello. He couldn't articulate his dread. *I am going on holiday*, he repeated silently. *People go on holiday.* Though his father was the only member of their family who had ever been abroad.

His leaving was a series of moments. Eating slowly the night before he left. His parents too relieved to notice that he barely spoke. His mother wanted to cut his hair. They did it outside now, taking a kitchen chair into the yard, the strands drifting away for the birds to make nests with. Edward said no, his hair was neat enough.

On the train, he felt tight-throated. Each jolt of the carriage landed in his stomach. A few years ago, he and Jack had been placed in separate classes at school and he had gone home, pulled the poker from the fire and touched it to his palm. The sudden impulse in him to know how that would feel. His dad had found him outside with tears on his face and his hand in a bucket of water. Edward called it an accident and his dad told him to keep his burnt hand in the water and count to ninety-nine. He had kept his hand beneath the table at dinner time, so his mother wouldn't see.

A girl came into his carriage on her own, with red lipstick drawn just outside the lines of her mouth. Sunburn spread across her cheeks and bridge of her nose. He helped her put her case up in the rack. She sat opposite him and pulled raisins one by one out of a cake, depositing them into her handkerchief.

'Where are you off to?' she asked.

'Paris.'

'How exciting,' she said.

He said, 'I suppose so.'

'You *suppose so*,' she said, funny but not unkind. 'Do you want my raisins?'

In a different story, Edward does call his sister.

She is no longer at the address he has written on his folded slip of paper. But a woman there comes to the phone with tea-stained teeth and a crown of curlers. She helps Edward find Agnes. The siblings meet beneath the white clock of a station Edward has never been to. They tell each other everything. How she had thought of her pregnancy like the tumour they both saw as children on the belly of a cow. A black, solid thing they found with their hands, parting the loose hair on its underside, after wondering why it moved so slowly, lumbering behind the herd as it ran across the field. An invasive growth. But one that could be expelled. They sit on the rug in her bedsit, though Agnes has two chairs, donated in a moment of uncharacteristic kindness by the upstairs neighbours. They talk into the night until the world beyond the rug feels less and less real. Edward looking down but being honest, tracing the zigzag pattern along the rug with the knuckle of his thumb.

But this is not what happened. Each was certain the other would turn them away and they withdrew completely from one another's lives.

As Edward moved away from her, his mother swept the floor of his bedroom. She stripped and laundered his bed. The sun threw her shadow onto the sheet as she hung it out.

When she had met Edward's father, things had happened in a way that felt both wrong and correct. As they worked together on the farm, the pain loosening from her body now that there was someone there to help, they became close. Once she had moved him – this man, this stranger really – into the house, it all happened outside of words. They were not the kind of people who could say, *Are you all right?* when they caught the other staring at nothing. Or the kind who could run outside like children when it snowed, laughing together with cold faces, noticing snowflakes land and dissolve in each other's hair. But Mary Webb could, by the time winter arrived, beckon Thomas Blood to the window as the field filled up with white. Him moving to stand behind her a question and her leaning lightly into him an answer. Her dropping her head to one side a question and him placing a hand on her left hip an answer.

Later, she went to church and sat in the gloom and confessed that she and Thomas had broken a trust and become close. In that way. She did not say the word *sex*. The guilt and joy of it, sun licking over the sheets, a snag of animal hair trembling on the barbed wire outside. It did not cross her mind that Father Flet, who had brought this man to her, might not be entirely surprised. But there were lots of things Edward's mother didn't think of. She moved like a person travelling through a heavy snow: head down, seeing only her own feet fall one after the other on the ground.

'You've got to be Tom Blood's boy,' said the man Edward met at Gare du Nord. 'I'm Malcom Merrill.'

Malcom Merrill's hand was overly warm and very firm. He had small, watery eyes and a square-shouldered French wife who laughed at everything Edward said. They took him back to their apartment and were kind, excited to see him. The couple seemed to have made up their minds before Edward arrived that he was going to be a very funny person, *like his dad*. But the person Mr Merrill recounted seemed nothing like Edward's father. That evening as they ate, Edward tried to imagine his father's big body moving fast, his face youthful, jokes tumbling from his lips. Mrs Merrill poured more wine into Edward's glass as Mr Merrill said, 'He had hidden it in the glovebox!' and exploded into laughter that made him shake his head, like he might choke, tears streaming from his eyes.

Edward tried hard to picture his father as the kind of man who would made those around him chuckle before he had even spoken, his presence promising entertainment. But he could only conjure the image of him silently carving ticks from his forearm with a knife at the kitchen table. Merrill produced a photograph of the two of them together in uniform and questions swam into Edward's brain. Was losing your hearing like diving into water and never coming up again? Had his father ever felt the cold metal of a gun in his hand, stood so close to another person he could see the open pores on their nose, the pink edge of the lower eyelid, and shot?

Edward got drunk that evening, for the first time in his life. Becoming drunk was lovely, his stomach unclenching and the tension falling out of his shoulders. But realising he was drunk was horrible. Bolts of paranoia shot through him. How had he been sitting? Had he been talking too loudly? When he rose in the night to vomit spectacularly into the toilet, Merrill seemed overjoyed, calling him *Tom Blood's boy through and through*.

He fell into a cottony sleep that lasted into the middle of the morning of his first day away. A white cat wandered into his bedroom and lay on his chest. With his fingers on the cat's fur, he thought of Jack's eyebrows and the tiny, pale hairs on his earlobes. Jack's small, neat ears somehow seemed connected to his singing voice, which was precise and clear-toned, though not very loud. Edward's mind lay flat, all the moments equalised, so that when he tried to think of one thing, other irrelevant things leaped out – how his sister had driven a pin through the flesh of her ears before she left home, the fact she would brave that pain not once but twice. He felt exhausted, drugged. His friend was far away from him.

He spent five weeks in Paris, reading in parks and burning things on his hosts' balcony when they were out. A Mediterranean-looking man with curls of thick hair like a baby goat smoked on the adjacent balcony, sunglasses catching in the light. Edward bought a packet of cigarettes from the newspaper kiosk and began to smoke with him. They never talked, but sometimes the man waved. The movement was as powerful as if he'd laid a hand on Edward's face. He'd wave back, but immediately have to look away, up to the collapsed chimney stacks or down to the pavement, a cluster of nuns gliding along it, the traffic conductor coming home from work in his shining hat.

He tried not to think of Jack. Away from home, Edward

could almost believe that in the few seconds in which his mother had opened his bedroom door and quickly closed it a few weeks before, she had not seen his body touching Jack's. He could almost imagine that later that day when he'd looked down from the bathroom window and saw her outside, normally such a colourless person, swollen and red-faced, pushing tears back into her eyes with the sheet she was holding, that she was crying about something else.

On his final day in the city, he noticed a sign dangling from a building: a metal bird with scissors for a beak and wings made of combs. He strode into Coiffure Hommes in an act of reckless confidence. He knew he didn't have the words for this interaction after the first line, and even that – *Une coupe de cheveux, s'il vous plaît* – was probably a little off what real people said. Then again, he wouldn't have known the script in his own language. The man who greeted him was his neighbour. The baby goat.

'You're the English boy,' he said, and Edward wondered what about him had given this away as they smoked on the balconies in silence, before realising he must have heard him speaking to Mr Merrill. Had this stranger listened on purpose?

He sat Edward in a leather chair, which his body felt too long for, his knees bending with his feet placed on the rest. He placed his fingertips on Edward's shoulders. Edward straightened his spine and placed his hands on his thighs, and then changed the arrangement, resting one on top of the other in his lap.

'Relax,' the man said, and Edward found that he could follow this instruction. He laughed.

'Sorry,' he said. 'I have never done this before.'

'Had a haircut?'

'Someone normally cuts it. My mother. Normally. When I am at home.'

'I can tell,' the man said. 'It is uneven at the back.'

His sleeves were rolled to his elbows. As he cut, he caught Edward's eye in the mirror sometimes. Flash of his scissors. Flash of his teeth. When he was finished, he placed his hand on the back of Edward's neck and held it there, like a mother dog's gentle mouth. The man moved his fingers slightly and met Edward's eyes in the glass.

Afterwards, he walked through a cool arcade and kept walking as the city grew dark. He could tell the Merrills he had got lost. Edward noticed his refection in the window of a bar and crossed the road to meet it. He saw a tall young man, thin, with freshly cut dark hair, framed by an arc of golden letters on the glass. He was consistently surprised by his height, but something else shocked him. How clear the lines of him were. How much of a person he was.

Decades from this moment, Edward would clear his parents' home and find a photograph from his final year of school. The choir. He would scan the faces, all the boys with their hair parted on the same side, looking for Jack's and then his own. He would be shocked at them both, at Jack for having spots on his cheeks, and at himself for looking, if not handsome, quite striking and serious, his dark features like something outlined with an illustrator's fine-point pen. He was not the gangly, provisional sort of person he had felt himself to be.

Some people in the bar pointed at him and giggled and he felt embarrassed for gawping at himself. He moved on.

A smell in the air suggested rain. It occurred to him that Jack was the only person in the world he really knew the smell of. He knew the smells other people carried – the tallow soap his parents scrubbed their hands with – but not the smell of them. He would see Jack when he went home. It felt good to decide it. He would tell him about the bird market full of metal cages, about the huge, long streets lined with trees. *Lined*, like a coat is lined, or a page, sharp pencil travelling across the paper along a ruler. Edward had spent so little time in cities, it was strange to see nature used decoratively, frivolously like that. Jack would understand what he meant.

His father collected him from the station. The farm seemed small, a place he would soon leave. His mother stood in the doorway. He remembered hiding as a child, the way she sometimes told him off and sometimes smiled as she drew him out, like it was a game they had decided together. The joy then of seeing light in her face. He neared the doorway. It was him now, reaching in. Her, being drawn. He had brought her a wheel of cheese. Their hug in front of the house was to be their last for decades.

Edward would not touch his mother again until 1987, the year of his grandson's birth. Visiting with a photograph of the baby, he would find her very old and weak, and see blankness spread through her, making her stand frozen in the kitchen with no memory of why she had gone in. Then Edward would go up behind her and guide her to the sink, her plait, white, hanging between them down her back. He would turn on the tap and lift her hands into the water, operating her like a marionette. She would laugh, quietly, girlishly, as the warmth of it softened the pain in her fingers.

He discovered that his best friend had moved away.

Some said *hospitalised* with a little twitch in their face. Sometimes Edward dreamed of electric shocks, of placing his hand against the fence that kept in the cows. Holding it there, letting all that power run through him. What did it feel like, he wondered, to lie down in a hospital and wait for someone to send a current through you? Buckles round the ankles and the wrists. Was waiting the worst part? Knowing it was about to come? And afterwards, did it linger with a dull or sharp taste? Did it tremble through you, glitches of it buzzing into your nerves, making you drop your keys or suddenly hurl your drink out of the cup – a streak of coffee dripping down the wall? Or was it a total experience, felt afterwards by its absence, the way land pushes so hard against you just by lying flat when you get off a boat? Maybe after such tension, everything felt too loose in you. The limbs jelly. The tongue dead inside the mouth.

In the future, when Edward meets his wife, her mouth will be pale pink. He will observe her in the school staffroom, taking a lipstick from her bag and reapplying it after she has eaten her sandwiches. The textures both sticky and powdery. He will wonder if kissing her would taste like licking a stamp.

Part Two

Joe & Emily

2012

Your treatment began. But it wasn't the end of ordinary days. We all put on shoes, and our fingernails continued to grow.

I understood that chemotherapy entailed you sitting for hours in the hospital in Birmingham with a drip in your arm, and that it would weaken you, so it was important not to see you if I had a cold. You went on alternate Tuesdays and it sometimes left you vomiting and vomiting afterwards until you had to go to A&E.

In a slim gap between recovering from one session and attending the next, you visited and sat at my kitchen table in Stoke Newington eating Turkish bread. The room smelled sharp and lemony from the antibacterial spray I'd swiped over the surfaces before you arrived.

'Jesus, Emily,' you said, laughing, 'your flat smells like a morgue.'

On the front of my fridge, a photograph of Solomon was printed streakily on a sheet of A4. He was standing in a waterfall. Across the paper, he'd written, *Happy Valen-TIME!* in black pen. I reached into the fridge for the milk, lifting the carton to my nose to make sure it wasn't sour.

'Chemo is awful,' you said, your face hidden from me by the fridge door. 'They're only doing it to convince me that I'm ill.'

'I can never tell when you're joking,' I said.

'Oh, pretty much always.'

The next day was a Thursday: 8 March. Your twenty-fifth birthday.

I had ordered a piping bag with different metal nozzles from the internet, and spent the morning making you a huge cake. Light flowed into the kitchen, and the flat was pleasantly quiet with Solomon at work. Soft sounds of the sugar and flour pouring. Sweetness in the air. The click of the butter knife hitting the board. As the cake cooled, I made two colours of icing, one pink and one red. I lifted my finger to taste them, then took a teaspoon from the drawer instead. I felt a small gimmer of pride to have thought of your immune-supressed body and protected it from my own. I placed my laptop on the counter and I did my best to copy a Chinese man on the screen as he demonstrated spooning the colours into the bag and piping them into roses. He smiled because his roses were so beautiful. Then I crossed the city to our parents' house with your cake heavy on my lap. On the train, a woman opposite met my eyes and grinned as I lifted lid of the box to check it was safe, uncrushed. At her feet, a grey rabbit crouched, twitching in a crate.

As I approached Mum and Dad's, our uncle Eddie's car pulled onto the drive. It was shiny, ostentatiously small and low to the ground. Grandad climbed out, his long body seeming to unfold as he leaned forward and straightened to rise from the passenger seat. He had a bunch of daffodils in his hand, which he lifted and waved as he called my name.

'Remind me,' he said, the question familiar from childhood, 'do you hug?'

I had asked Mum about it many years before, because other relatives would just seize our small bodies and plant kisses on our cheeks. She told me that her father came from a family that never hugged. Before that, I had never considered that such a thing could exist. I hugged him. I could feel the daffodils against my back. Clean, familiar scent of his coat. I had not seen him since your diagnosis. The sudden urge to cry. To stay with my face against the smooth fabric. He wouldn't comment, I knew. Wouldn't touch the dark patch of tears. Would just say something like, *It's waterproof*, if I tried to apologise. But neither of us lingered in the hug, and my eyes were dry when it ended.

It was warm inside the house. By the time I took out your cake, it had spent a little too long near the radiator and the sugar and the butter had begun to separate. The surface looked grainy, and my piped roses had slightly slid from their places. You seemed both happy and uncomfortable as we sang around you, shadows on your face from the candles. Grandad's singing voice was resonant and deep, more definite somehow than the one he spoke with. Dad moved his lips inaudibly. Uncle Eddie was happy and loud and tuneless. Distracted, Mum trailed a beat behind. You blew the candles out, squirming under the attention. No one told you to make a wish.

We had beautiful parties as children. Mum laid bright cloths on the living-room floor for us all to sit on. Dad bought plain iced cakes, rinsed the watercolours from his brushes and painted pictures on them in food colouring. Mum did puppet shows, crouched behind a cardboard box, throwing glitter on us when the fairy appeared like the pyrotechnic snap in the pantomime. Dad did magic. Once, between tricks, he paused to peel an orange. As the skin came off slowly, we all shrieked with delight because it had an apple inside. It was the most incredible thing we had seen in our lives.

This year, you had dozens of presents. Far more than normal. That evening, you sat on the sofa opening them, after Eddie and Grandad had left. Your friends and teachers sent you CDs and books. You opened an envelope and photos spilled across the floor – Canadian landscapes, printed by Harriet. Mum came in with hot chocolate, a tiny orange mark on the rim of the cup where she'd smuggled in some turmeric. Sitting beside you, she pulled our grandmother's engagement ring from her hand.

'Joe,' she said, 'you should have this. I know you like antiques.'

You slid it onto your little finger for a moment, then held your hand to the light to admire the line of small rubies. Then you removed it and slipped it away into your pocket.

Dad had printed a book of photographs in which things looked like other things: shadows in swimming pools and plastic caught in trees, trapped in the branches like bright blossom or fruit. I was reminded of the set of photos he had taken years ago when we got a dog, Helga. She was actually luminously white if you parted her black fur. Dad posed us with her each Sunday and the collection revealed the process of her growth in a way we couldn't see at the time.

I had knitted you a scarf, even though it was spring. It was cream and blue with a twisting pattern down the front and slightly shorter than it should be because the wool was so expensive.

Each gift was a little wish. As if we could persuade you, or some unknown entity, that you were important enough to live.

The next day, you came into Central London and waited for me outside my university. We strolled down Oxford Street and you bought a jumper, cancer rattling all around us, coins into collection buckets and yellow daffodils pinned to people's chests. That night, I dreamed about rats. White rats beneath my floorboards and burrowing through the mattress under my back.

A week later, your treatment was suspended. Suddenly. The shadow in your lung – inconclusive on the initial scans – turned out not to be cancer but tuberculosis. A stranger had coughed into the atmosphere near you and droplets had travelled into your airways.

'But we were vaccinated,' I said to Mum.

I remembered how your arm had bled and blistered with infection after your BCG. It had hurt and left tiny red bloodstains on the left sleeves of your school shirts. Two years later when my turn came, our parents and even Grandad showed me their discreet scars to assuage my fear that my body would react as yours had. I waited in line outside the school hall, then sat before the nurse. A swipe of antiseptic, the needle pushing in, a cotton ball pressed onto my arm, held with tape. Jesus looked on from the wall. Later in my classroom, I noticed a clutch of cotton balls from several different arms, clustered in the mouth of the plastic bin, each with its pinprick dab of blood. I was fine. No infection, just a small, flat mark. Yours, even now, was raised, the skin taut and slightly shiny.

Apparently, the vaccine did not always work, did not always last. I lifted my arm in the shower, twisted it round to see the little scar.

I feel like I should be writing letters to my lover fighting in the Crimean War, you texted me.

At least TB is glamorous, I texted back.

I called you. We joked about pale beauties coughing bright blood. Keats. Nicole Kidman in *Moulin Rouge*.

'The consumption,' you said. 'Hand me my handker-chief,' and you issued a faux-delicate cough.

Chemo would be paused. You'd had just three sessions.

You told me you were eager to get back to it but sound-ed relieved and I pictured you lying very flat, above the covers on your single bed, your limbs thrown out wide. Solomon had told me once that taking a punch hurts less if the body is relaxed. But we naturally brace against attack. I pictured the tension seeping from your body now. Fear floating up. Dissipating. You'd been given a reprieve.

'One thing at a time,' Mum said brightly, the next time she and I spoke.

Weeks passed. Dad visited you and sent me an email update with a photograph. The TB drugs were gentler than chemo but were turning your skin red. His subject line was *Mr Tomato*. Everyone seemed strangely jubilant. The tuberculosis clouding your lungs had been discovered early and was treatable. People had stopped dying from it in this part of the world.

When winter seemed long over, it snowed in London: thick, settling on the ground. I thought of our first winter in Derbyshire, all the snow blinding us, our faces pink and pinched and awestruck in the photographs. The real world at last living up to *The Snowman*. It was the end of March. Two and a half months since your diagnosis. I had to be checked. Because you were a twenty-five-year-old vegetarian whose organs were behaving like you were in your seventies and ate nothing but red meat. Perhaps there was some trigger lurking in our genes that made sense of that.

I had been to the hospital near our parents' house just once, a few years before – I'd smoked a joint at Glastonbury and stood up too long in the sun. My faint, face down into the grass, coincided with the exact moment that the strobe lights came on, so everyone panicked and thought I had epilepsy. That time, I went alone and a large, businesslike nurse placed electrodes all over my breasts with little stickers. I laughed and told her, *This is so weird*. The consultant's verdict afterwards: *It looks like your GP has got into a bit of a flap*.

Now, I came with Dad, through the melting snow, hungry after forty-eight hours without food, though I had been permitted small servings of jelly. A nurse fitted a canula inside my elbow – 'You'll feel a scratch' – and sedative seeped in. I could feel the cold of it travelling through my body. My muscles relaxed. I was wheeled into another room, where they slid a camera into my anus. A nurse held my hand because it hurt. For a few moments, I saw pictures on the screen. Colours and heat and shapes inside my body. The movement of being wheeled back out woke me briefly and then I fell back into a heavy, beautiful sleep. On waking again, I was given the most delicious sandwich. Dad took a photograph of me sleepily eating it. He pulled into a supermarket soon after we left and bought me a bottle of wine, because, he said, 'That can't have been much fun.'

We continued the drive quietly. Schoolchildren on the pavements, their black shoes churning the remains of the snow. Inside the car, warmth, music, guitar notes climbing gently over each other. A soft voice hummed and sang words in a language I did not understand. It felt like a lullaby. The song was very long. When we arrived in front of the house, Dad left the engine running to keep the radio on. The snow had almost melted. Patches remained on the heads of the stone animals in the neighbour's garden. A crown of white between the otter's ears. We sat still together, the melody and the car's gentle vibration filling the space. I looked at Dad. He had lost weight, the flesh stretching between his cheekbone and his jaw. He turned and looked at me as if to speak when the music stopped. But then we just got up and went inside.

When I returned to my flat, I shouted at Solomon because the place was a mess. A cave with the curtains closed. Beer cans full of cigarette butts, dropped in with a fizzling sound as the dregs put them out. I hated him.

That night, I slid out of bed and went into the kitchen. The light seemed incredibly bright when I turned it on. I stood still on the tiles, then opened the cupboard and took out two wine glasses. I smashed them both into the sink. I wondered if Solomon had heard, his eyes open now in the dark on the other side of the wall. I waited, but he did not come in. The shards shone. I wanted to squeeze a jagged piece of glass into my palm, knowing I would not be able to explain it, wondering where I could do it, if there was somewhere on my body where it would never be seen, reminding myself that I was twenty-two and not sixteen.

You came home from university when I broke up with my first boyfriend – a boy your age with shock-blond hair whom everyone called Milky Bar. He worked in the Co-op in the marketplace and used his staff discount that day to buy an enormous bottle of Cointreau, reappearing briefly at our house afterwards in time to throw it up all over our sofa, which for ever afterwards smelled of bile and oranges. And I took a pink disposable razor and drew it in little stripes down the skin of my forearm. I knew a girl who did it all the time, taking out her compass in class and puncturing her flesh. I thought I would give it a try – experimental violence. I suppose I was very upset, but all I remember is going to find Mum in the pub, bringing her outside and pulling up my sleeve. *Oh dear, Emily*, she said. *Oh dear*, and she took me home to bathe my arm in saline.

The next day, your knock on my bedroom door woke me. The dog's lead was in your in your hand. *What are you doing here?* I asked, and you said, *Mum told me you were upset.* You waited until we were on the hill to ask what was wrong. The dog dug her way beneath a stile. *Nothing,*

I said, my sleeve pulled down to my wrist. *You know how Mum overreacts*.

I broke several glasses during your illness. Wine glasses were best, their bowls breaking instantly, quietly against the side of the sink, their stems intact in my fingers. I would have liked to hurl them at the floor, but I never did that. By the morning, I had always gathered up the pieces and put them in a plastic bag in the bin.

You continued the TB treatment into the end of April, when it was declared safe for you to restart chemo after a month and a half off.

Soon after, Dad and I moved you out of your room in Birmingham. You had tried to push through, but it wasn't working. You sat in the car as we gathered all your things. Neat stacks of music and museum postcards removed from their tessellating positions on your pinboard, along with a printed list of concerts and, for some reason, the label of a beer bottle, *Tsing Tao*, peeled off very carefully and flattened out. If I had tried to do that, I would have peeled too fast and ripped it. Your trainers and one pair of smart shoes. Your jeans and jumpers and one suit. The books by your bed, a drawer full of underwear and, beneath that, two condoms and a sachet of lubricant in a cardboard envelope with the name of a bar on it. Your violin, buckled into its case, stood on end in a corner.

We loaded your stuff into the boot as you waited, too weak to help, patient as we dismantled your life. There was nothing to say to you. I folded in the silver arms of the music stand. A small parade of jade animals lined the lip of your window. A monkey, a tortoise, a pig and a bear. Dad folded each one into two squares of toilet paper and placed them in the pocket of his coat.

Another person was going to have this room. Maybe someone living in a flat who had missed their chance to get into halls. Someone with condensation on their walls and a growing patch of black mould on their ceiling, who would go to student services and not believe their luck when they were told this place had come up. Or maybe it didn't work like that. Maybe it would simply sit empty until the end of term because you had already paid for it.

You had been told they would help you readjust when you came back. You had tried to keep being there, but you weren't turning in your work. You were lying on this rough carpet, vomiting into the bin, poisoned by treatment, when you were meant to turn up to tutorials. We took your calendar off the wall and drove you home to Mum and Dad's.

The prototypal journey is with our grandparents, not our parents. Grandad, his sleeves shortening as he reaches for the steering wheel. Grandma slipping her shoes off into the seat well and placing her feet, bony ankles in tan pop socks, on the dashboard. These voyages were always to somewhere exciting – the pantomime, the armoury in Leeds, where I wept with fear at the gap between the steps – and they survive so much more distinctly than our daily trips with Mum and Dad. At traffic lights, Grandad would reach down and open a two-litre bottle of flat own-brand lemonade, take a swig and pass it into the back for us, asking, *Do you want some fizzy?* and it was uniquely delicious because we weren't allowed that kind of thing at home.

When I was four and you were six, we were left with them for a week. Grandad gave us a small patch of his vegetable garden and crouched in the dirt beside us as we combed through the soil, removing pebbles and twigs. We planted carrots in rows, then gathered small rocks from all over the garden to build a border round what was ours, while Mum and Dad dismantled furniture, wrapped objects up in paper and closed boxes with brown tape, moving out of our London home. I wonder if they touched hands for a moment when they had finished packing, stood in the doorway perhaps and gazed into the denuded flat, proud perhaps, that there were two new people in the world since they had moved in. Or perhaps just a glimmer of a wish, that they were packing up for an adventure that didn't involve us. Or no final moment: they were too tired from scrubbing every trace of use from the walls and still swearing at each other because she hadn't taped the bottom of a box before he had picked it up and precious things had fallen out and broken – a mug of his father's, her great-grandmother's china dog.

I can picture us at the end of that week, travelling toward the home we would grow up in. Night-time traffic reports cutting into the radio news and our grandparents throwing sharp little complaints at each other and ushering up encouraging stories and questions for you and me. They argued about the temperature dial and Grandma won and the windows steamed as we crossed the moor, lurching at every bend so we arrived at our new home exhausted and excited and pale with nausea. *This*, Grandad told us, *is where you live now.* Our new home had a real fire, which you could look at but had to stand a metre away from, the safety zone marked by the edge of the rug. It had a blue sofa, left by the previous owners, which Mum had found a pair of dirty knickers inside when she lifted the cushions.

After that, they took us each summer to the seaside. The vibration below us changed as the road became the gravel of the caravan park. We swam and slept side by side on fold-out twin beds and returned, suntanned, after a week to our parents striding out to meet us saying, *We missed you! We missed you!*

One day, once you had turned ten and we were permitted to cross the road to the sweet shop unsupervised, as long as we held hands, we slipped next door into a joke shop, where we acquired a rubber vomit. It sat on a shelf in the gloom beside whoopee cushions and dummy cigarettes with ends that glowed if you sucked them. We felt so clever on the night of our journey home, waiting for our moment. The moor stretched out either side of the road like a dark ocean, and you brought out the vomit, a small, irregular oval of yellow rubber with chunks of brown in it, and laid it across my cupped hands. We grinned at each other; then you yelled, *Emily has been sick!* Grandad calmly began to pull over as Grandma swivelled in her seat, peering at us in the dark and passing me her handkerchief – *Oh, Emily, never mind.* I felt your deflation next to mine. It was disappointing, wrong – as if someone had sat on a whoopee cushion and simply said, *Oh, excuse me,* and carried on eating their breakfast.

But now I see it, their kindness. I had been sick and

they would deal with it. My body was not an outrage to them. There was no need to make a fuss.

When we were children, you never, ever fell asleep in the car, however long the journey. Sometimes I would wake up on a motorway with you next to me, eyes open and back straight, staring out at the trail of tail lights in the dark. But now, as we carried you away from the life you had made in Birmingham, you fell asleep in the passenger seat beside Dad before we were out of the city. Surrounded by your possessions, I was the one wide awake in the back.

I woke early the next morning and made coffee in our parents' kitchen, a few black dots falling onto the pale countertop as I poured out the grounds. The first gulp of it burned the roof of my mouth. Dad came in and sat next to me at the table, instead of opposite. He kept his voice low to say, 'You know, we mustn't pressure Joe to have treatment.'

I felt a quiet thud of adrenaline but said, 'Yeah,' as if I had also considered this.

'Because we could have a really nice year together,' Dad said. 'I think—' He drew silent at the sound of Mum descending the stairs. She was humming.

She came in and heated half a cup of milk in the microwave, then darkened it with coffee. Dad asked her why the house was so hot and she said she wanted it nice and warm for you when you woke up.

'It's too much,' he said, tearing off his jumper. 'Joe will be uncomfortable.'

'All right Mark,' she said, standing quickly and opening

the cupboard to pull out plates, 'Emily, do you want some toast?'

The cutlery rattled in the drawer as she opened it. I slipped my thumb into my mouth to touch the coffee burn, the skin papery from it, tearing into tiny white strips. I could feel the architecture of my mouth. Ridges supporting the roof. I accepted the toast. As she made it, Mum told me you were responding well to chemo.

'They can really blast him because he's so young and strong.'

Dad left the kitchen and moved noisily through the house, turning down each radiator. He never finished his sentence.

I left before you got up. I did not know what to do with what Dad had begun to say, and by the time I reached my flat, I had put his words away, like objects kept, but on a high shelf or deep in the basement: things with no everyday function. It would have felt disloyal to you to hold them any closer.

At home, Solomon said a letter had come. It bore the emblem of the hospital where I had had my colonoscopy. I used a knife to open the envelope, sliding it through the paper slowly. The letter said that I was normal. The procedure had concluded that my insides were fine.

May. A sudden burst of hot days. Smiles and naked limbs in the streets. The year's first wasps.

One afternoon between classes, I went into John Lewis on Oxford Street. Mum had given me a hundred pounds to buy a posh airbed, so you would have something to sleep on if you ever stayed at my flat. After I had bought it, I rode up and down on the escalators for a long time, not wanting to go back into university with a huge department-store bag. I pictured my friends asking, *Why do you have so much money?* and me replying stupidly, *Because my brother might die.*

Sometimes I did not want to go over and see you at Mum and Dad's. I did not want our family. Sad, sceptical face of our father. Mum, deflated, lost. I wanted to stay in my part of London, with Solomon, his hair tied back, sitting on our bed playing the guitar. Our separate planet, an hour and ten minutes of buses and Tubes and trains away from family. To swim up and down for hours in the tiny pool of the ladies-only gym, where Orthodox women hung their wigs on the pegs in the changing room. I wanted someone to spill boiling tea over me in the café at the end of my road, so that I could cry in there and no one would think, *Oh, that poor girl has been dumped.* I glowed with jealousy for the teenagers who came in and sat around drinking lattes, pretending to be grown-ups.

Sometimes Mum or Dad called and I did not want to answer. Did not want the news.

'Can you talk to him?' Mum said. 'He's sleeping with his razor under his pillow.'

You shaved with a cut-throat razor – an affectation,

really, but you got away with it, like many things, because you indulged it quietly. Your love of old and ornate objects extended to figures carved from jade and ancient coins, but you dressed plainly and would never have grown a retro moustache, twiddled between the fingers with special wax. When I asked why you didn't use a normal razor, you shrugged and said, *Because this one is beautiful.* Now I imagined the sharp edge of it, folded away into its sheath, tucked inside the pillowcase, the pillow's cloud of feathers, your head resting on top. I thought of the princess and the pea. *No*, I thought. I did not want to go over. I was pissed off at your quiet melodrama. The illogic of it. I wanted to be alone with Solomon.

But I did go. The house had accumulated many boxes of tablets, a yellow bin for medical waste, special plastic bags that were a fierce green colour. I sat with you on your bed. The room was more fully yours than it had ever been before. You had cut a black-and-white photograph of a cellist from the newspaper and tacked it to the wall above your headboard, and I was happy to see your music stand erected in the window, with a piece upon it, the staves standing out on the slightly translucent page. The jade monkey crouched on your nightstand. I wondered where his friends were.

You leaned back and opened your palms. 'I just feel so out of control.'

You placed your hands over your face and slid them downwards, like you were smoothing out the skin.

'OK,' I said.

Your expression was flat, but you balled your hands into fists at your sides.

'It makes sense, Joe,' I said slowly. 'Of course you do.'

Maybe you should be allowed the cold, safe feeling of your life being your own to end.

'But, Joe,' I told you, 'you're scaring Mum and Dad.'

The following day, I went with you for treatment. You were surprisingly buoyant when Dad dropped us at the hospital, the previous night's sadness vanished from your face. You knew the woman at the desk and greeted a man in the corridor and another on the ward. It occurred to me that you had stepped into this world five months ago and perhaps felt a little pride at guiding me through it, big brother again, explaining how it all worked, as you had done each time I moved schools.

'This is my sister,' you said to the nurse.

We joked that your arm was like Swiss cheese as she looked for a vein.

A woman near us on the ward had a series of procedures that ended in her wearing a strange sort of padded helmet for the last hour. I kept looking over wondering what it was for, whether it meant her cancer lived somewhere inside her skull. When she was allowed to take it off and go home, she said to the man with her, 'Does my hair look bad?' running her hair through her fingers until the nurse told her that touching it too much would break it. I imagined having fibreglass hair on my head, brittle, snapping off into sharp little ends.

We chatted about Harriet's new boyfriend, how it would be weird if she married him and had kids with Canadian accents. Then we attempted the crossword from the newspaper, until you closed your eyes, wincing, and stopped responding to the clues. I read articles aloud to you. Then I read them silently. For the last bit, neither of us did anything.

That evening, as we waited in the hospital entrance for Dad to bring the car round, you looked so cold. I draped your coat round your shoulders, so that you would not have to slide your damaged arm through the sleeves. You were silent as I did up the top button.

'Capes are in,' I told you. 'You look like Sherlock Holmes.'

You went straight up to bed at Mum and Dad's. I brought you a tea, but you didn't want it. A new sensitivity made the heat too much for your hands. We laughed lightly at your attempts to hold the cup. Then I got on the train to cross London. Out of the suburbs and into the city and out to the other edge. All the black shapes of the buildings were covered in little rectangles of light against the dark blue sky. I sat sealed into the train, wrapped in my cardigan with my jacket draped over my naked knees. The warmth of the day had fallen away in the dark. For a moment, it was wonderful to be with no one but strangers.

Dad texted me to say you had begun throwing up.

Why are you telling me this? I thought.

Again and again, he messaged. *I have never seen anything like it.*

The term drew to its close. I bought new pens and ran the words I would write with them through my brain. All my swallowed quotes and facts. Time to perform. I thought of secondary school, the sallow-faced, bleeding Jesus at the front of the hall. The moderator who had attempted to eat a packet of crisps during my biology GCSE, placing each on her tongue and closing her mouth slowly to silently dissolve them. *Body of Christ*, you had joked. You did exams in a separate room with a grey-haired woman who transcribed your dictated answers. You hated it, being singled out because your letters scrambled on the page.

But your consolation was music. Your specialness. At school, you accompanied the hymns on the violin Grandad had bought you. You played the swooping descants in assembly, with a mixture of abandon and complete control that made me feel self-conscious. Me in the choir, though I could never really hold the harmonies. At your proper concerts, the dark wood of your violin made the other instruments look shiny and orange. I noticed that the people who fidgeted through all the rest of the music sat still for you, and that the other parents looked at our mum and dad with a combination of suspicion and awe.

You had your performance and – though I attempted for a while to dance, encasing my body in green Lycra for a year of Wednesday nights and scolding it for galloping left when the other girls all galloped right – what I had was this: weeks of neat facts on index cards, then curving my back over a page and scratching out answers until my hand ached. It was mine. You the performer and me the reader, the student. Enjoyably confounding because you were so shy and I talkative. It was as if we had arranged ourselves like that on purpose, to never block the other's light.

Good luck, you texted me. I entered my exams with a floating feeling. A bubble in the back of my brain that might lift me from my seat.

As I began, your vein was punctured open and you sat for hours with drugs dripping down into you. Attempts on your life. What lovely aches I had by the end. Cramp in the centre of my palm. The feeling that I had been gripping my jaw. All the other students concentrating in unison. Togetherness with no one allowed to look at me. The pleasure, for three hours, of forgetting all about you.

In July, your skin broke into spots. Quickly. A side effect of treatment. You were apparently responding well – your scans seemed promising and surgery a possibility – but a new drug had been introduced. Your body was in shock.

Dad said, 'He's dressing like a Mexican bandit.'

We met outside the British Museum, bus fumes and summer heat. You had a hat on, and the scarf I had knitted was wrapped round your face. You laughed at yourself but seemed sad and remote. Raw-looking bumps marked the exposed skin, the visible strip of forehead, your cheeks and nose, the skin around your glasses. They were different to the spots you had had as a teenager. Violent. I thought the museum might not let you in all covered up and you would be humiliated and angry. I could not let that happen.

'Let's go for a walk,' I said. 'Let's go to Covent Garden.'

I moved you quickly down the street. 'Let's go in here.'

I led you through the door of a make-up shop and to a woman with sculpted eyebrows and a big hairdo under her hijab. White bars of light round the mirrors and the cool of the air-con.

'My brother is having some trouble with his skin,' I said.

I couldn't look at you, in case you were cross with me for taking over.

She smiled and put you into a chair and turned her attention to you. No fuss. She dotted lotions on your palms for you to put on your face and said that she was getting you to do it yourself so that you would remember the steps. I think she knew that you might think she was afraid to touch you.

'This will even out the texture,' she said.

You sat in the tall chair, surrounded by women, and said, 'This feels nice,' as I pretended to look at things.

She dusted powder over your face – 'Just to take the redness out' – and then another powder – 'To set it.'

Then she turned you toward the mirror and you smiled. You bought the make-up and we went out. Your scarf was in your bag and you held your hat. The woman had been serious but light and I wanted to tell her, *You are an important person*, even though she was just selling you things.

In the museum, the air-conditioning flowed over our skins and everything felt ordinary. It was a wonderful day. I had fixed something.

Imagine it. The flash of light across a London pavement the day our parents met. Her in a red scarf, singing herself down the street. Her hair is cut close and hennaed. Him, hung-over, the heat giving him a headache, but out anyway, with his camera, trying to capture a pane of splintered glass.

Just a flash of light, really, between that day and the four of us sitting side by side, a family, on matching chairs in the handsome geneticist's office. The appointment was at Guy's Hospital, the place where you and I were both born.

Today, you looked healthy but thin, which made the whole thing seem abstract. The geneticist asked questions and pulled a piece of paper from the draw of his printer, on which he drew a map of our extended family. The mole removed from Uncle Eddie's back five years ago. The death of Dad's aunt when he was a child. The branches spread as Mum and Dad spoke. A little cancer, no more than average.

The geneticist looked down at what he had drawn, frowned and said, 'Looks like it's random.'

'He was fit, wasn't he?' I whispered to you as we walked away from his office down the stairs, our parents a few steps behind.

You shook your head at me, but a smile threatened to break over your mouth.

'Well?' I said.

'Yeah, he was fit,' you said.

'What are you two laughing about?' Dad said, as the hospital doors slid open and released us out into the light.

As I travelled home, I watched two women and a little boy, sitting a few rows ahead of me on the 149. One had white hair, flowing onto her back from beneath a blue hat. The other, sat across the aisle, was a little younger, or seemed it because she had dyed her hair pink. The child was between them, his legs swinging, turned out over the side of the seat, not touching the ground. They were caught in his orbit.

I thought of Grandma long ago, saying, *Joe could charm the birds out of the trees.*

The boy twisted round, whispered in the older woman's ear, then reached up and very carefully took the hat from her head.

'We have to close our eyes,' the white-haired woman said solemnly. 'He is going to disappear and come back as somebody else.'

Bodies could be saved.

At some point in our childhood, we began to be given small animals. We were told that they belonged to us and that we must feed them and touch them gently. We loved them and gave them names. In the evenings, we would fill their water bottles at the kitchen tap and take them down to the bottom of the garden to their hutch. They clipped on upside down, their metal spouts poking through the lace of chicken wire. When they sucked, we saw how narrow and sharp their teeth were.

Reality was malleable then. Our real animals, with real ribs and lungs and darting eyes, were only subtly different from the stuffed toys in our bedrooms. Those also moved, but only when you weren't looking. I had pleading conversations with them, trying to draw out their trust enough for them to blink or raise a soft limb in front of me. We tried to catch them out by bursting back into a room suddenly just after we had left.

One evening, I put my teddy bear under a reading lamp to warm him up and screamed when I smelled smoke and pulled him out, the ears and fabric scalp burned off. The fluff inside his head had singed and melted into lumps. He smelled of fire and chemicals as Dad took him away, saying he would fix him.

Dad did the same when a rat moved in with Mozart, your guinea pig, and bit him on the cheek and he went bald, first round the bite, then all over, and eventually died from stress. We ran with his body, the scrap of him with his patches of skin and fur, up to the house, banging the kitchen door open as Dad stood at the stove. What was wrong? we demanded. Why wouldn't he move? There was steam on the windows. Very calmly, Dad dried his hands and tore two paper towels from the roll. Suddenly it felt like we should stop shouting and be very quiet. Dad placed Mozart's little body between the towels. If there was a breath or a blink, a moment in which he summoned this gentle, false reaction, it was too quick for us to notice it. He held the animal and said he was very poorly, but he would see what he could do. I felt almost excited, my breath involuntarily holding at the possibility of a rebirth, as he took Mozart away into another room. He had brought my teddy bear back from the basement, healed, with a yellow fishing hat stitched firmly over his head. This time, he just said, *I tried.*

Trying was its own kind of magic.

One night in the caravan, Grandad told us the story of a puppy born dead. He sat beside Grandma at the fold-down table, speaking quietly, his hands resting on the Formica, and told us of how, when he was a boy, his friend's Labrador had whelped six puppies and one had come out not breathing. They had put it in the oven, which was not hot, just warm, from the last meal cooked in it. The story stayed with me. I would sometimes ask him to retell it, delighting in asking questions I knew the answers to: *Were you really there? Did it really come back to life?*

Eleanor

1958

Here comes somebody else, Eleanor. She is the last to fully enter this story and will be the first to leave it. Miracle of this woman crossing a carpet. She is thirty years old. Small. Her cardigan could fit a child. She takes a seat in the staffroom, as she does each weekday, and withdraws a sandwich from her bag. The window frames her as she eats, and with each bite she leaves a faint print of lipstick on the bread. Edward Blood walks in. Eleanor tells him his lace is undone. She changes his life completely. Because of this moment, new lives will begin.

But what about her life? It must be noted that Eleanor has not lived in a straight line toward this moment. She is here by chance.

1931

Here is Eleanor's first memory. She is three years old and around her lies an expanse of grass. Her father places his palms beneath her armpits, his fingers curving round her ribs. He lifts her. Then flight, the world rushing into her lungs. He throws and catches her. She feels a joyful panic before she falls back into his fingers, safety flooding into her through the heels of his hands.

1946–1971

Eleanor arrives in Bangor at eighteen. A new adult, though she looks younger. The city is small but bigger than home: a modest town two hours away by train. The mountain and the water give it scale. Here, there are more people, and also more earth and more edge. A clutch of sharp pencils and fine-tipped thoughts in her brain. A case of clothes and blank workbooks. A blanket from home for the bed.

She shares a hostel with other girls from the college, shakes hands, smiling, and makes room in herself for their faces and names. *Gwen, Nina, Elwyn, Edith, Beth*. Her little rectangle of a bedroom is the first she's ever had to herself. She is the oldest of six siblings. Her childhood saw new person after new person placed into her lap, their downy skulls soft against the skin of her palm, always someone there to share space with, a small brother or sister to comfort or crouch in front of – *Fly away, Peter. Fly away, Paul* – vanishing her thumbs behind her back. Now, she closes the door of this room she will not have to share and listens to the quiet as she runs her fingertips over the walls.

On the first night, the blanket heavy on her, she wakes

to the sound of a woman screaming outside. Muffled. She knocks on Elwyn's door. Her new friend listens for a moment; then a smile breaks over her worried mouth.

'Oh, that,' she says. 'Eleanor, that's just a fox.'

She learns. Teacher training is subtler than she thought. The new intake are told, the first time they sit and hover their pencils above their brand-new books, that teaching isn't just the distribution of knowledge but the creation of atmosphere. It's conjuring an environment by how you arrange the seats and modulate your voice. A performance. *Yes*, Eleanor thinks, *a big story*. She is living in a bigger story than people might think.

Life inches out and out. She slips on high heels and grows. Learns the stages of children's forming brains, learns to frame her face in curls. Meets men. *Ivor, David, Geraint, Reg*. Ivor asks her out and she says maybe. But *maybe* means *no*. She sits in the cinema with Elwyn and Nina on either side, light splashing their faces, just knowing there's someone else for her, someone taller and more certain than him.

That December, they all go to a dance. Breath pluming from their lips as they walk down from the college into town, heat and music flushing over them as they get through the doors. The small hall sweats and moves to the five-piece band. Eleanor has a borrowed blue dress on with a dart pinned into the back, sucking out the space that Elwyn's bigger body flowed into.

The crowd doesn't really part, but it feels like it.

By the time she sees him, over Ivor's shoulder, he's

already looking at her. A paper decoration falls from the ceiling and touches the back of her head on its way to the ground. It is whipped up for a second before it is crushed under people's feet. A smile blooms over his mouth when he sees her notice him. Black hair and a dinner jacket in this hot room where all the other men are just in shirts. A smile spreads up the backs of her legs. He knifes through the pairs, takes her from her partner and begins to dance. It might seem rude were he not beautiful. But he is. Not tall, like the man in her imagination and in her future, but with a sort of confidence that fills the space. It's a difficult step, but he's sensed that she can do it. Childhood lessons sit inside her body: dancing over church floorboards that sighed up and down as she crossed them, ribbons wrapping her ankles, the stamp and rattle of tap shoes, music in her legs, her steadily acquired knowledge of how to grip her stomach – the clean stretch of self between her hipbones and ribs – but keep her outer layer soft, of how to rise onto her toes and smile demurely as her feet bled. Other men would nervously tell her, *You're good*, as they moved round the room and she'd feel this hopping, twitching energy, because she was better than them and they always wanted to lead. But he doesn't say anything, except, *No*, when another man reaches out to take her hand.

He leans in and with his face close she thinks about the process of shaving. She had often watched her father do it, sitting on the edge of the bath as he stood by the sink, his hand flat on his chest to pull his neck taught, a slow stroke of the brush, then three quick ones.

As they dance, the pin dart in her dress comes undone

and begins to cut her skin. They agree to meet the following week.

Eleanor is so happy that evening that there is a little
scrape of sad in it. The band, the horns that sound like animals crying. A warm touch in a cold, raining place. Back
in her room, she grinds soap flakes into the blood mark in
the dress and goes at it with a nailbrush, like she has learned
to do with bloodstains in her knickers. She straightens the
bent pin. She had felt the two of them drawing looks from
around the room as they moved across the floor. Space
being made for them. Slow, slow, quick, quick, slow. Two
dark-haired, elegant people. She withdraws her hairpins
and gets into bed. The weight of the blanket. Dim light
sleeking under the bottom of the curtain. Now she's small
again. Not much body at all under her thin nightie. But
tonight, she had been something to see. The best in the
room. The best one.

There's a shadow down the High Street where the mountain casts its body over the town. Eleanor arrives at the
café first and wishes they had decided to meet beneath the
clock. That way, she could just walk off if he didn't come.
She sits at the bar, crosses her right leg over her left. Feels
tiny in the high seat, far from the ground. Keeps her back
straight. Counts the black tiles on the floor and the lamps
above her head. Imagines one of the glass orbs falling and
smashing on her plate. Tries a few arrangements of her
hands. Every time the bell goes, her head snaps to the
door. Cold air and strangers. Then he comes in with a
long coat on and she forgets, entirely, to be self-conscious.
Her body breaks into a smile.

'Hello,' he says, taking off his hat.

How did he shape the word as if there was already a joke between them? Like it was a code, a reference to something else. Black hair, black belt, black shoes, black watch strap. He looks around and lifts an eyebrow at the place.

'We should sit at a table,' he says, flashes a smile and drops his tone, steps closer. 'I'd rather look at you than Melvis,' indicating with a glance the fat, flat-footed waitress.

Eleanor slides down from the bar. Click of her shoes over the tiles. He pulls her chair out, brushes his seat with the ridge of his palm and places his coat carefully over the back so that the fabric hangs evenly, the shoulders don't collapse. Then he's opposite her. His chest under his shirt. When he orders the tea, he flirts, just a little, with poor Melvis. (Is that her real name, or is part of the game inventing a name for her?) It's not much. A little shift in his bearing, a slight lowering of his voice, asking what *she* would recommend. But he keeps shooting his gaze back to Eleanor, and Melvis isn't sure if she's being flattered or mocked. Music somewhere. Spoons against white cups. He brings out a cigarette case. Silver that must be stainless steel.

'Do you smoke?' he asks Melvis first, tapping one against the table and passing it up to her.

Eleanor feels a laugh rise in her as the waitress flushes and tells him, 'Oh no, no! I'm working,' and hurries away.

She feels like a conspirator. Catches his eye when the cups and cakes are put down a little too fast, a clatter and a tremor over the liquid. And it feels like life with this person would be all jokes, and the jokes would never be on her.

His name is Henry. He's twenty-eight. He has a magician's timing and sense of how to direct attention. An almost feminine ability to see himself from the outside, to look away, then look intently back so that the circles of hazel round his dark irises are noticed. Perhaps he's looked at himself in the mirror and thought the effect similar to a solar eclipse. Eleanor won't realise for a long time that when he pays for these cups of tea and two cakes, he has planned for her to see just how many notes are in his wallet. That afternoon, she keeps forgetting the mountain and thinking the sky is overcast. Expects to see raindrops on the glass. And then they step out and it's cold but clear. He puts his arm through her arm. They walk out to the pier. He kisses her when they say goodbye, brief, but confident. On the mouth. And she runs, as soon as she is alone, has to put the energy somewhere. As she reaches the gate of the hostel, a tiny piece of her tooth comes out. She folds it, the first in a series of little breaks, into a handkerchief and keeps it in her coat.

It is very difficult, as she gets to know him, to separate Henry from his beauty and the special things that seem to spring from his fingers. Meat and sugar. Sherry. It's like magic, but really it's just money. Money and knowing who to ask. Months pass. Eleanor becomes a girl with extra bacon. It feels like a trick when he produces an orange and a knife to peel it. Oil releasing as the skin breaks. The pith and the pips in her mouth. Shards of flesh. Not wanting to wash her hands.

A bad thing happens. They pause on the way to a party to pick up his coat. Or put it down. Something. No one is there. He turns on a lamp. Her shoes hurt, so she sits on the carpet. Why not the sofa? She doesn't know. It cuts a better picture perhaps, her stockinged feet tucked to one side of her on the rug.

Afterwards, there are tears on her face, and Henry says, 'It's all right,' and kisses them off.

'I'm sorry,' Eleanor says. Everyone she knows apologises when they cry.

Before this, the blunt, silent weight of his body on her, her back on the carpet, no words in her throat, turning her head away, pushing his hands, her skirt scrunched at her hips, his fingers undeniable round her wrists. Blankness. Blankness spreading through her. A tear in her tights. A little break inside her body. But never mind. Hadn't she sat, just an hour before, proud to be beside him in the cinema, her heart shimmering through her blouse, a stripe of light above them, willing him to place his hand upon her thigh? After that she feels a tiny but permanent clench at the centre of herself, though her surface stays the same.

The next day, he takes her to meet his mum. She's elegant like him but doesn't make it look easy. Long, filed fingernails. Dyed hair. Eleanor gets drunk on preserved plums and throws up as soon as she is alone. A slick of vomit over the rubies in her engagement ring.

She qualifies as a teacher and marries him, at the church in her home town. Her parents are proud. His money flows through her in the shape of her dress. Her new mother-in-law wears a dead fox. Photographs. Her sister and a sulky five-year-old cousin in matching frocks at her sides. The tiny shower of sound as handfuls of rice land all around them on the ground. And Henry. Like a film star. That night, she thinks of the bad moment and knows that she has fixed it. By loving him. That night, she breathes deeply and loves the smell of his body in the dark.

How embarrassing that a person like that would turn out to hit you. The first blow happens suddenly, and in the moment after it, she sees herself as if from the outside. So little. Bafflement on her face. Looking up at him like a child, as if it were about to be explained. It was different to the way he'd pushed her onto the carpet. Couldn't that be love, passion, something that arrived from some hidden point of good? But a hit could only mean harm. What else could a hit mean? They argue. She struggles to find a job.

'You don't need to work,' he says. 'I don't want you to work.'

But she keeps looking and keeps her new learned knowledge close, rereads her notes and speaks them silently to herself as she washes up. There are moments of levity. Dances. Card games and a reel of jokes. But to find yourself scanning the room for things to defend yourself with — the intrusive thought that the black ashtray could be smashed against the side of someone's face, to find yourself mapping the movements it would take, which person would reach it first — that is no good.

There isn't a final straw. Just a little clutch of bruises and the sight of her shoes waiting for her in the hall. Black against the coral carpet. The knowledge, very calm, that she could slip into them and go.

Home for a bit. An exploded blood vessel in her eye.

But really nothing to show. The brothers and sisters back around her. The pub chucks an old piano out and her brother wheels it home. Fag ash falls into the keys. *Handsome is as handsome does*, they all say. Almost like they know just what has happened. Her mum touches her a lot during this time. A hand between her shoulder blades, a hand on the arm. Eleanor feels reclaimed. Only sometimes flinches.

Her little sister takes her for a walk and says, 'Don't tell the boys about it. Don't tell Dad. They'll kill him.'

They pull blackberries off the bushes, check for spider webs and grubs, and place them into their mouths.

Divorce. Eleanor is twenty-three. She feels marked. But she also feels better. An envelope falls onto the doormat with a lump inside. There's no letter, just the rings she slid off as she left. The plain gold band and the engagement ring with blood-red stones. It feels like a threat.

'Keep that one,' her mum says. 'You'll not get one like that again.'

There are too many teachers in Wales, so in 1954, she moves over the border for a job in a school. And then there she is, in a cardigan and skirt, framed by the board. Chalk on her fingertips. Her life keeps spooling out. Her shadow along the bottom of the swimming pool. How do we remember violence once it is over? In our willingness to stiffen, to suddenly be ready to be hit. She is all right. Only sometimes turns sharply and finds that no one is there.

Eleanor sits by the staffroom window with her legs crossed at the ankles. In 1958, Edward Blood walks in, the knot loose on one of his laces. His hair is dark like

Henry's, but not quite black. Tall. Slim hips. He is dressed *quietly* in a brown suit.

He nears her to take a book from the table and she says, 'Your lace is coming undone.'

Edward flushes. Perhaps there is a little power left in her.

'Sorry,' he says. 'I mean, thank you.'

Day by day she begins to learn about him in little pieces. They sit together on the blue staffroom chairs. Edward likes music. No, he doesn't dance, but he sings. Eleanor begins to detect on him the faint smell of chorine.

One day, she comes out of the swimming pool as Edward is going in. She feels self-conscious that her hair is wet, and she thinks about this feeling on the way home. That evening, she presses her bottom teeth hard against her top teeth and sends the nose of a needle into a loop of white wool. A knit stitch. She reverses the action for a purl. She swallows and rearranges her feet under her on the chair. She thinks about Edward as the glove grows.

In the hallway outside his classroom, the click of her shoes slows and falls silent. Edward's voice comes out clearly through the inch gap of the door, a small gap between the words and the sound of him chalking them onto the board. The anatomy of something – *Calamus. Rachis. Scapus. Vane.* He mumbles in the staffroom. This other voice, this confident person, is a revelation.

She goes to watch him sing, looks for him in the line of other men, serious, sheet music in front of him, ready to begin. Edward is taller than Henry, but less sure in his body. His hair is fine, prematurely receding, where Henry's had been thick. He is younger instead of older than her. Uncertain. She knows that she can be the one to lead.

For a short time, she tries to will the thought of kissing her into his brain. Then she just does it. They are outside, horse chestnuts on the ground in their cases of green spikes. He stiffens, then relaxes. He takes her hand. Absolution. The coolness of his fingers.

They drive out to Wales to meet her family. Noise and colour. So many of them. Slurping, bashing their spoons against the sides of their cups. They stop at Colwyn Bay on the way back, tear a bun in half and sit by the water, breathing the salt air. Nearby children ride up and down the sand on a mechanical elephant. It is gentle-looking, folds of fabric round its feet and half-closed eyes. She is shocked when Edward says that he liked her family. *How can he*, she thinks, *everyone bashing elbows at the table, no conversation finished before another is begun?* But when they visit his parents, she understands. As they arrive, something tells her that she has dressed all wrong. She slides off her red scarf, wipes her lipstick into her hanky. She is dressed, she realises, for Henry's mother, who made her want to seem like an exciting person. But everything in the house Edward came from is plain. His father is serious and almost silent in a deep-backed chair, his weathered fingers resting impassively on his legs. His mother is also quiet but fast-moving. Swift but graceless like sped-up film. During the visit, Eleanor's eyes keep returning to the china dog on the mantelpiece: the one extraneous object in the room.

Edward and Eleanor laugh madly all the way back in the car, swooping quickly down into the valleys so the rainwater splashes up around them, tears falling from their faces like children. It is the relief of being out of there. At the end of this journey, Edward places his hand over hers. Henry would have taken it, held it firmly in his, but Edward reaches out so gently that she could easily pull away. He leans in and kisses her. A small kiss. His mouth on hers. He raises his eyebrows at her when she pulls away and they laugh again. She knots her scarf below her chin to guard her curls before she gets out of the car.

A second wedding. A second go. She pops the ruby engagement ring back onto her hand and pretends it's an heirloom. No bridesmaids – no, thank you. Afterwards, when they get into bed, Eleanor lies there, waiting, expecting a sudden, quick movement. Braces herself for the grip. Then she sits up and watches him. His long spine and the curls of hair at the neck of his pyjamas. Edward is asleep. She moves close to him, puts her head on his chest. Her feet throb, glad to be out of her shoes. It is a relief to rest. She remembers her first night at college, the screaming voice of the fox. Eleanor wakes on the first whole day of their marriage with a circular button mark in the flesh of her cheek.

The planting of their first garden. Trowel a little earth out, press in a seed. One day a small shoot, another day a leaf. Water and love them and wait for what's next. She plants flowers, and he plants broad beans and potatoes.

'See,' he says, 'a proper farmer's son.'

She says, 'We're not getting a cow.'

At night, they roll into each other and latch on like baby apes. Need. Not for sex but nearness. It is a relief to love him less. To live in a suburb and walk together to the school. A shared box of sandwiches. She begins to habitually count things. Touch this twice. Touch that once. Touch the space between your temple and your eye on the left side of your face. She wears pale green. The red ring glinting secretly inside an oven glove.

When they do have sex, the nearness between them goes. Edward holds her tightly but keeps his eyes closed. As if he has vanished. His body is on her, in her, but somehow, he is elsewhere. She would like to be reached for. To have her neck licked and her nightdress lifted. Even a hand over the mouth. But when it does happen, it is never like that. Sometimes she slips into his shoes at night and walks around the close. Just walking. Pausing in the dark spot between islands of light where one of the bulbs has blown in the streetlamp.

Eleanor feels capacity in her. In the stretch of self between hip and ribs where another person could be made. First a miscarriage. Blood in the bath. Edward kisses her palms. Touches her back. He says, 'We'll be all right,' and folds her into a towel like a child.

Henry would never have done that.

They get a dog. Eleanor runs her fingernail along the seams of green pods, uncasing grey-green broad beans sleeping side by side in a row. She drops them into a bowl. Her belly blooms outwards again. Keeps going until there are silverfish rips in the skin. A stillbirth. A story travels out from this moment, gets absorbed into the family. A baby born with a distended neck, taken by the doctor and preserved somewhere in a jar. Can that be true? Their child whipped away and suspended in formaldehyde. They call her Ruth. The little swan.

A third pregnancy. Underwear and nightie in a bag by the front door. But not quite allowing themselves to believe it. In 1961, Eleanor has a baby girl, who screams and screams so you can't not listen. She uses the name again. Ruth. Why waste it? This Ruth lives. Eleanor brings her into school to show the children. Everyone around them like a show. She walks out with her child into the sunshine and doesn't go back to work for five years.

The first winter with the baby is biting cold. On all the doorsteps, the bottle tops rise above the bottles on columns of frozen milk. Edward smiling, his lips pale in the cold, reaching into the pram to readjust the blankets. His choir sing the *Messiah*, and he looks to her in the audience as he takes the bass line of 'For Unto Us a Child Is Born'.

A year later, they have Eddie. Another child who lives. *It is amazing*, the doctor says, *what the body can do when the mind looks the other way.*

Part Three

Joe & Emily

2012

There was a time when we said *cured*. Cautiously. The on-cologist said it had worked, that you had been delivered. The tumours had shrunk to almost nothing. *Remission* didn't cover the progress made. It was September. The final weeks of the summer break before the start of term. Dad phoned to tell me, and I asked him to repeat it.

Cured.

What was he talking about? It was beyond the realm of what I thought could happen. I tried to absorb the word and thought of meat hanging up in big basements. I placed my forehead on the door of the fridge and shut myself against the full force of the miracle. The relief would be too great. The sigh would deflate me.

A day later, I met you in a huge bookshop. You were waiting, as we had agreed, at the bottom of the stairs. I was five minutes late. You beamed as you saw me. We hugged. In the café, you chose a bright red slice of cake from the illuminated cabinet. We shared it. Taste of coffee. A red crumb lodged under my thumbnail. Sugar on my hands. It felt like a birthday. We talked about the rest of our lives.

I would like to leave us here. September sunshine. Not warm but bright. You would have the operation. Not to trim out the cancer but the place where it had been. Then they would seal you up.

The end.

The world seemed the same. People on the bus still smelled of sweat and perfume and chicken shops, but you were going to live.

Bodies could be saved.

One evening after school at Harriet's house, her father tried to explain his pacemaker to me. He seemed proud of it, animated. Everyone was eating sausages and peas, and I was eating peas. I kept saying, *Really?* Because I couldn't imagine it at all. Eventually, he unbuttoned his shirt, slowly. He was older and there were white hairs on his chest. I could see a faint shape beneath his skin. *You can touch it*, he said, and nodded. Then he picked up my fingers to trace the pacemaker's rectangular outline. *Dad*, Harriet said. She squashed her peas beneath the tines of her fork, shook her head and said, *He does this all the time.*

But I was amazed.

I went on holiday and you had the operation. I flew through a soft white sky. I held hands with Solomon on the beach and the scalpel slid in while I was elsewhere. It was the end of summer. In Spain, the grass was tough. I wore shorts with a piece of paper in the pocket on which I had written the numbers from *uno* to *diez*; *Me gustaria . . . un vaso de agua, un vino tinto, una cerveza; Soy vegeteriano; Qué hora es?* I was not even going to see you in hospital, wires in your body, surrounded by machines. By the time I returned, it would be gone.

I stood in the sea with my eyes closed. A patch of cool blue in the hot, hungry world. I thought of how I would move the furniture around in the flat when I got home. How I would buy stationery and bright white underwear, and everything would feel brand new.

Solomon led me through a fish market, holding my hand to keep me with him in the crowd. The dead fish seemed beautiful to me, luminously silver, with their open mouths and blank faces. We stepped out into a side street and he beamed, 'Here it is!' gesturing at a small café, proud to be the one who'd read the guidebook.

Inside, it was peaceful and dimly lit. The sun threw shadows across the floor, arcs from the curving backs of the chairs and the *Rac* from *Desayunos Raciones*, which was printed across the window. As we sat, I noticed Solomon's nose and cheeks were slightly red.

'You're sunburned,' I said.

He grinned and said, 'You know I never sunburn.'

'Honey, you can say that all you like but it still won't be true.'

We ate bread and shining olives. Solomon scrunched

pink pieces of ham with his fingers and brought them to his lips.

'Let's go travelling next summer,' he said.

I imagined the two of us in humid unknown cities. No one near but strangers. Maybe we could do that. He began to talk rapidly about how we'd save the money. He could take extra shifts and I could work in a coffee shop at weekends and over Christmas. You could eat like a king for three pounds a day in Vietnam. Or we could go to Colombia. Colombia was meant to be amazing. I'd love the jungle and all the art.

'I want to,' I said, quietly.

He said took my hand and said, 'I know it depends.'

'Yeah,' I said.

'You know,' he said, 'I feel like I haven't properly seen you since we went to my dad's.'

I thought of the three of us driving along the coast in Northern Ireland, back in January, me on the back seat with my palms under my thighs, watching the back of Solomon's neck as he'd grappled for shared ground with his dad. Seven months had passed since then.

He signalled for the bill and said, 'It's just, I've kind of missed you.'

That week, we ate yellow rice and both got sunburned and drank too much beer. In the afternoons, we had sex in our cheap hotel room, and at night, we lay in bed scrolling through our photographs. A dog on a sunlit pavement. Solomon asleep in a deckchair. His cigarette, poised in the ashtray, smoke rising, beside my tiny cup of espresso. We didn't talk about travelling again, but we barely spoke of you either, except to acknowledge Mum's message immediately after your surgery: *Joe out of operation. Tired but fine.*

'He's been through it, hasn't he?' Solomon said, and raised his glass as if to toast you.

Two days before our departure, I woke up early and lay looking at Solomon as he snored in his white T-shirt. His naked legs were tangled in the sheet. I reached out and touched his hair.

I wondered who the last people to sleep on this bed were. A couple. Perhaps they came away together to find out what was left between them, closing their eyes and telling themselves that when they opened them, they needed to imagine the person in front of them was someone they didn't already know every shape and line of, every gesture. I pictured them going for dinner in the evening and walking separately along the beach with the big, dark sea beside them. Perhaps it was in this room that their certainties had turned into questions. Did they want to be naked together in bed or should he put on his T-shirt? Should their bodies touch?

I kissed Solomon's forehead lightly as he slept. He did not stir. Then I rose from the bed, crossed the room and crouched to where my phone was plugged in at the opposite wall. I had received a text message. I opened it.

Emily. So sorry about the news. Try not to despair. Big hugs xx.

The flaccid language. Big hugs and two kisses from a friend of Mum's, who would have typed slowly, squinting at the words as they formed. Her fingers with pink-painted nails too big for the touchscreen. When we were little, the boiler had broken at home and warm water had spewed from it into the bathroom and this woman had come round to look after us as our parents panicked and pressed towels into the leak and took turns to be on the phone.

Try not to despair.

I left a note for Solomon that I'd gone for a walk, though I knew he wouldn't wake up for hours. Sitting at a plastic café table, I phoned home, raising a flat palm as if to say, *Don't you dare*, to a man who approached, smiling, with bright plastic sunglasses and woven bracelets.

'We're just a few steps back,' Mum said.

They had opened you up and found more cancer. Hidden. She told me it was still going to be all right and I wanted to believe her because I was on holiday and there were two days left and I had gone into my overdraft to be there.

Behind the hotel was a patch of woodland carpeted in brown pine needles. I went there to stand beneath the trees. I thought of the fairy tale of the girl who walks the world in iron shoes to find her sweetheart.

When I came back, Solomon was sitting up in bed. I explained things.

'Right,' he said.

I felt like I was letting him down. He would have to hold me again as he had on the nights when I cried into our pillows at home and there was no end to it, except exhaustion. The body completely empty. He put his arm round my back.

'What if we didn't go home?' I asked.

We returned, my sunburn already starting to shed. Solomon brought me a gin and tonic on the plane even though it was expensive.

He smiled weakly when I said, 'At least this time, I know the bad news already.'

I went straight from the airport to see you, and Mum kept making more coffee as soon as we finished our cups. She brought in crackers and asked if we wanted to watch a film. She had picked all of the Cape gooseberries from the pot in the garden and Dad shouted at her because they weren't ripe. You seemed thinner. I asked you about violin, but you said you had stopped playing. It hurt to hold it, chemotherapy heavy in your veins. I washed up and Mum came in. She put her hand on my shoulder and told me she was still optimistic. I wanted to turn and push her onto the floor and hear a bone snap.

On the train back to North London, I messaged Harriet. I made phone calls to our other shared friends, so they would not assume they had for ever to visit you.

People could die.

When we were children, Dad mentioned one night that as a boy, he had seen another boy drown in a river. He was sitting at the kitchen table after dinner with the dog in his lap. The story was exciting because it was like something from a book or a film, but when we began to ask questions, he just looked cross and said he actually didn't want to talk about it. It felt unfair that he would bring something like that up then refuse to go into it.

University began again on 24 September. Back to school.

I got off the Tube at Oxford Circus. Folders in my ruck-sack, notebooks and pens. As the train slid away into the tunnel, it revealed a poster on the curved wall: models in bright knitted jumpers holding up paper signs on which they had written wishes in fat black pen. One read, *I wish for a puppy*, and another, *I wish good health for my family*. A blonde model peered out from behind her piece of paper, hair tumbling down, smiling with a fashionable gap between her front teeth. My eyes stared at the words and my legs slowed but kept moving. I couldn't look forward. My breath still and my chest locked, not able to expand or deflate.

Then a woman barged past hissing, 'Watch where you're going,' and it was broken.

I hadn't even seen her face, just her dyed red bob, that hard cherry colour people put over dark hair to make it shine. A prickling feeling, then tears. I was going too slowly to knock her hard, so it wasn't that that had an-gered her, but the fact that I had broken the contract, London's unspoken agreement not to break pace. I turned and followed her, skipping to catch up as she marched down the platform.

She turned, surprised, when I touched her shoulder.

'Excuse me.'

She took out an earbud and said, 'Yes?' in a gentler voice than I had expected.

Angry, hesitant, trying to sound sane, I asked, 'Are you the woman who said, *Watch where you're going*?'

'I did, yeah.'

'It's just that . . . just . . .' I gestured to the poster and tried to explain.

She tipped her head to one side and said, 'I'm sorry if I upset you,' put her arm on my sleeve and squeezed as the Tube arrived. Then it took her away.

I stayed there for a moment and wondered if the models had even written their own wishes or had had wishes handed to them. Maybe the signs were blank, the wishes added later. Then I walked quickly to the exit, weeping, humiliated by her kindness.

Grandad came to London. He had stopped driving long distances but announced to Mum that he would make an exception. We joked about him upstaging you by having a car accident.

It was the start of October. He arrived on a Saturday afternoon with a plastic bag of broad beans from his garden. The last of the year. He was early and Mum and Dad were still at the shops. You were resting upstairs. Grandad came through to the kitchen with me. It was unusual for the two of us to be alone. I made coffee and we shelled the beans into a large bowl. I slid my thumbnail along the seams of their casings. He sat opposite, squeezing the pods gently, then opening them like books with his thumbs. Pale green. A white scar running along their sides.

'How's university?' he asked.

I stalled and realised people had stopped asking this. Then I said, 'It's fine,' feeling a twinge of annoyance. He had misplaced the centre of my life.

But his face was open across the table. He wasn't just asking for something to say. He and Grandma had always asked us detailed questions about school. Because we had no other grandparents, it took me a long time to realise that their interest came from having been teachers; education was not simply a universal preoccupation among the elderly. He stopped shelling for a moment and slowly opened and closed his fingers. Little marks all over his hands. Age spots. A perfect stripe of scar through one palm. You had been talking less and less about returning to your course. I glanced at the ceiling. You wouldn't be able to hear us.

I told him that I'd have lots of essays this term but no exams. Slid briefly into the lovely mundanity of it, the

facts falling lightly like the beans into the bowl. My sched-
ule. The little dramas that only brushed the edges of my
life: the girl caught for plagiarism, the lecturer who had
confided, *I was psychotic when I last taught this course*, as we
chatted at the traffic lights after class.

'Good Lord,' Grandad said, laughing, his eyebrows
shooting up for a second. One of his eyebrow hairs was
completely white and stuck out like a whisker from the
rest.

'And what about your friends?' he said, taking a sip from
his coffee cup, and I felt a sudden sharp longing for Harriet
as I told him that yes, I had friends at uni but no one that
close. No one like her.

'Well,' he said, 'best friends are different, aren't they?'

Above us, music turned on in your room. I dropped
my voice and told him how I had sat with my tutor and
explained the situation with you. How I had cried, then
joked that I'd have to dry my face so the students lined up
outside her office wouldn't think it was her fault. She'd
joked back, *Leave it. Everyone thinks I'm too nice.*

Grandad laughed at that. Then he said, 'This is very
hard for you.'

'It's harder for Joe.'

'In a different way.'

He and Grandma had always worked hard to make
me as special as you. Once, as I looped the caravan park
aged eight or nine, my arm taut in front of me as the dog
pulled on her lead, I saw them standing with one of their
holiday friends outside the caravan, listening to you practise through the thin walls. The woman wore a baseball
cap over her white hair. *Amazing*, she said and they all

beamed. *And this is Emily!* Grandma exclaimed as I neared, as if this too was amazing. *It is helpful of you to walk the dog*, Grandad said. I sat down by them on the grass to listen to the rest of the concert you did not know you were giving.

We resumed our task. Each broad bean landed in the bowl with a tiny sound. Mum had cut all the buttons off Grandma's cardigans after she died. They clinked against one another as she dropped them into a jar. *You can't make a museum*, she had said. *You just have to keep something small.*

That night as Grandad and Mum watched television and Dad washed up our plates, I sat upstairs on the end of your bed. You were above the covers in your pyjama bottoms and a T-shirt with a black outline of a bird on it. Your skin was getting yellow.

'Do you remember,' you said, 'how I hardly drank when we were young?'

A flash of memory, of you coming to the rec to get me because I had been sick on myself and Harriet had called you, the way you lifted my arm and slung it round your shoulder to walk me home – *For fuck's sake, Emily* – trying to keep your own clothes clean.

'I should have gone for it,' you said, 'seeing as my liver is failing anyway.'

You laughed softly. I wanted to say something.

'I don't think you missed much, Joe. Those weren't my proudest moments.'

You smirked. I hoped you weren't remembering something too bad.

'Do you remember when you kissed Andy McGregor?' you said.

'I don't know what you're talking about,' I said.

You said, 'Sure,' and I said, 'Oh God.'

You exhaled.

Downstairs, Mum and Grandad were watching *Casualty*. The sound of a siren and someone shouting leaked up through the living-room ceiling, through the cavity between floors, through your floorboards and your bedroom carpet. How, as our lives became more and more about illness, scans, needles, tubes and tablets, could they watch something set in a hospital?

You were looking at me. You said, 'I just feel like I have missed my chance.'

'To kiss Andy McGregor?' I asked.

Then I said sorry, even though you had laughed.

You climbed into bed, saying you were not tired, just cold. It had grown dark outside.

'Are you all right, Joe?' I said.

After a pause, you said, 'Yeah.' Slow. Half asleep.

You began to breathe heavily.

'Joe?' I said.

You didn't answer.

I turned your lamp off and went out of the room.

I had grown up with such a desire to protect you. When you were bullied in primary school, I held up my palms in the garden and told you to practise punching them. Once, when we were teenagers, Harriet and I invited you into our realm, the place where we drank vodka, hidden behind the church at the end of her road. You were uncomfortable, giggling as the booze spread through you, reaching for the hedge and shredding the privet between your fingers. *Let's teach Joe how to be cool!* Harriet cried, and we grabbed at you like you were a marionette and altered your posture. *That's it – lean a bit. No, that's too much, Joe. You look like an old man.* And yes, perhaps we were a little cruel to you, but we were only making you ready for the world.

People could die.

One night, you and Dad and my boyfriend, Milky Bar, came to watch me dance in the clapped-out ballroom of an underoccupied hotel. I was fourteen. You and Milky Bar sat next to each other smirking, in a way that meant I had to pretend you were not there if I wanted to remember my steps. My hair scraped back and flattened down with palmfuls of cold gel, breasts shaking in my emerald-green leotard every time I landed a little too hard. Mum was not there. I kept looking for her, but afterwards Dad told me that she had been with a friend who was dying. I was shocked by that word, *dying*. It felt so adult to hear that instead of *ill*. But I trampled through it, because I'd never met this friend, saying it was better that Mum was absent. It meant fewer people to be embarrassed in front of.

In the subsequent days, Mum and some other women came and went from our house, drank wine and cried in the kitchen about Helen. Helen had some part of her throat removed a year before, the flesh replaced with something mechanical or electronic. Mum had returned from work one night saying Helen had been asked if she was a robot by someone who phoned. I had thought about Helen's children then, whom I didn't really know either, though I had met them: how strange it would be if your mum came home from hospital sounding so different, how your impulse might be to laugh even though you definitely weren't supposed to. Now she was dead. What struck me most was that our mum seemed so involved with this person that you and I hardly knew.

Autumn took hold, like always. My breath came out in curls and the world was full of warm light. It was the time of year when women wore new boots and black leather shoulder bags, when people liked to look in control, zipping themselves up and binding themselves in with scarves. I felt ugly. I felt full of dark green power, my veins overfull, resolutely healthy, offensively robust. It was about to be my birthday – twenty-three. Harriet sent me a long, narrow box of flowers through the post. Orchids. Each stem was stuck in its own tiny thimble of water. Flowers for me in drinking shoes. At home, I accidentally dropped a plate on the tiles and sobbed as Solomon quietly swept up the pieces. When we watched television, his hand was heavy on my thigh and he began to kiss me on the forehead instead of the mouth, like I was six years old. I spent a lot of time cleaning the fridge, and he spent a lot of time asleep. *He's hiding*, I thought, as the flat offered itself to me without complaint. I bleached things until my fingers burned. Asleep, Solomon could be there without being there. He did not have to look at me. I sprayed vinegar onto my reflection and wiped it away. I scrubbed off the black mould behind the bath taps with a toothbrush.

Miracles glittered everywhere, spilled out across the pavements. *Come on*, I said to them. *Come on*. I studied and ate noodles in the café next to the humanities building. Everyone in there seemed absurd, lonely: men in suits and women in dark blouses, eating boxes of leaves, being dignified. All of us sitting alone opposite empty chairs. I thought about how when I had worked in a call centre, a woman had told me, *Thank you, you have been magnificent,*

and I wondered what magnificent was. I thought about
how if you were out on your own in nature and you saw
a wheezing, wobbling animal, it would be kind to hold it
as it died. To be with it then leave the weather to lick the
flesh from its bones. A goat or something. I thought about
birds and goats. I thought about livers, bowels, lungs.

I almost wept in the marble lobby at university when I
couldn't find my student card. A day later, I felt nothing
when I reached into my pocket and realised I had lost
my gloves. White, knitted by Grandma, for herself, long
before I was born. *Goodbye gloves*, I thought. I pictured
them somewhere in the city without me, casing a stranger's
hands.

I began to miss classes. Just sometimes.

One day, I lay with you on the malting red rug in Mum
and Dad's living room. I was meant to be in a lecture taking
notes on Victorian novels. We listened to a duet for viola
and violin. When we stood, there were red fibres all over
our backs. Another day, I got dressed and put all the right
books in my bag, only to sit at the bus stop letting busses
pass. The choreography hadn't changed – the sequence of
movements it took to arrive in the classroom – but life had
a hole in it. I lifted my hand and used my teeth to push
back my cuticles. The bench was cold through my clothes.
It got later and later, until there was no point going in at
all.

I was trying to push through, but it wasn't working. My
life was absorbing into yours.

From the outset, my life was flanked by yours.

There is a photograph of us aged one and three, sleeping, light sliding over our bodies through glass. The kind of day that picks out all the dust in the air. My foot is in your hand. Our mum is a naked letter *C* on top of the bed covers. Her body is pale, flesh folding at her stomach. Dad wouldn't have thought about whether she'd want that captured, his photographer's instinct kicking in as soon as he entered the room.

There is a photograph of us standing on the balcony of our first home, naked and covered in paint, pressing green handprints onto the glass sliding door, balloon bellies and grins. How fine our eyebrows are, as if someone had run a toothbrush through them. A flash of paint marks your chin and lower lip, and I have been told that you bit me ferociously during this time, though you were getting a little old for experimental violence.

And in the unphotographed shards of my early life, my first memories, you are either present or somewhere peripheral, close. Our four legs kicking the bath water. Our sides and shoulders touching through pyjama fabric as we sit side by side on the sofa to watch *The Snowman*, wearing a white flicker into the VHS. We are frightened because we know in the end that he will melt.

Aged three, I got lost in a shopping centre and waited with a homeless woman to be found. The episode ended with you appearing, coming into my vision, your hand in Dad's. I was found and you were half of the party that found me.

It is strange to think that for you, it was not like this.

I was not an absolute. That you learned the world for

two years and seven months before I was in it. Thousands of tunnels burrowing through your brain, sparks in your synapses, before I even existed.

People could die.

One summer, we did not go to the caravan with our grandparents because Grandma was not well. I was twelve and you were fourteen. We were told she would not die, but she looked so different in the hospital when we visited her. Her hair was different, and she seemed bruised, although there was no injury, as if the bruise was happening on the inside. She seemed a step behind somehow, her readiness gone. Whenever we left the hospital, I didn't know what the last thing to say should be, so I just said, *Goodbye.*

It would have been a betrayal to say, *I love you.* It didn't belong there in the story where she wasn't going to die.

One Friday that autumn, we picked you up early from orchestra and drove quickly over the moor with Dad, arriving in time to see Grandma's body, dead but still plugged into a machine that made her seem like she was breathing. In the car, we had drunk apple juice, which made me feel travel-sick, and you seemed so still in the dark, your mouth closed and eyes unblinking.

I was so angry at you for not reacting.

We left Grandma's body and we went back to her house. All her things were in it. Her black handbag sat next to the sofa. There was a stack of VHS tapes beside the television. Someone ordered a takeaway curry. The smell and the sound of the food arriving, silver containers with edges that fold down to hold on the white lids. Heat rising from the rice. The television was on. Mum ate almost nothing, and Dad finished what was on her plate. Uncle Eddie was there. Grandad sat in the corner, not crying, very quiet. At some point, my plate tilted in my lap and orange sauce slid off onto the carpet. None of the adults noticed, so I went into the kitchen and wet a cloth to clean it up. The calendar on the wall was covered in appointments in Grandma's neat writing.

That night, we stayed there, and in the morning, Grandad took you and me to the swimming pool. He said very little. We all swam up and down for a while, then walked back through the park. When we got back, we discovered that no one had been told where we had been.

About a month later, Grandad had picked up Grandma's thick needles and tapestry threads. He'd finished what she had been working on. But at the framer's, they'd said it wasn't straight and he'd shouted, *It's the fucking Bayeux. It's not supposed to be straight.* It was true – she hadn't just made a mistake; he hadn't just continued her mistake – but Mum had to go into the shop and apologise, to tell them he wasn't normally like that. He took it home, framing it himself in the garage. He told us once that she came back from time to time to shout at him in his dreams.

And I learned to dance. I tried. I kept thinking of the day when Grandma had slipped our plates into the dishwasher after breakfast and drawn a chalk circle on the floor. She went upstairs and brought out a pair of old tap shoes. Black, with ankle straps. Tutankhamun's face glowered from the corner where it was singed from one of your T-shirts onto the plate of the trouser press. She stepped into the circle and showed me some steps, tapping neat beats, teaspoon on eggshell, firm and light. I could picture myself doing it, but when I tried, I had no grace. She smoothed the disappointment from her face and put away the shoes.

Later, I longed to tell her that I learned the stamp-hop, step-flap, ball-change, stamp, stamp-hop, step-flap, ball-change, stamp – *I like eggs, cheese and butter. I like eggs, cheese and butter* – of the compound timestep.

One afternoon in mid–October, I sat upstairs on my favourite bus: the number 73, which passes St Paul's. I saw a woman down on the pavement. A city woman with a suit on and straight black hair in a ponytail. She was walking along in the cold sunshine carrying a big paper cup. And I wondered what it would be like to be the one down there with the big cup in my hands. Fake snow inside a shop window, though there were two whole months until Christmas. Her on the pavement and me on the bus. Anything in the world was possible.

Here comes the miracle, I thought. *Hold tight. Here it comes, loud and blinding. All the animals and insects must clear out of the way. It is going to burn the earth.*

Eleanor

1966–1975

Eleanor stands, breathing behind an ironing board with over half her life left.

She chases the creases from a blouse, watching the news, tears falling down her cheeks. A slag heap has fallen on the children of Aberfan. Things collapse. She loses her accent. When her son is four, she returns to work and her pupils don't ask where she is from, though she still says *tooth* as *tuth*. She has absorbed her new home. She twists a rag in vinegar to clean the windows. Has a dog. Spits to clean the children's faces. She has done it: made a real life.

But sometimes it feels like there is a hole in it.

She feels drained and has stopped reaching for Edward in the dark. Giving her body to the children – feeding them, letting them pull at her as they learned to grab and stand – made it easy to never touch him. To not mind not being touched.

'I'm sorry,' she tries to tell him, willing him to mind.

Eleanor looks down at the red engagement ring sometimes and remembers she's survived. Her exit. Quiet. A bloodless release. Just a small scar. A small difference in her bearing. A small mark beneath the eye. Memory of cool fabric wrapped round her neck to hide three round bruises.

One day, she is in the car with Edward. They bicker about directions and he takes her wrist for a moment and says, *Listen*, and a feeling rises inside her – *Go on, break my bones*. But his hand is already back on the wheel. She looks in the mirror at the children on the back seat. Ruth drawing in the condensation on the window. Eddie working his fingers at the edges of a scab.

She drains boiled carrots and serves them in a Pyrex dish. Scrapes butter over toast. Feels an urge to look through Edward's things. For what? There's no apparent crime, just the sense of retreat in him. The creeping knowledge that she may not be the only one accepting second-place rosette. Takes her trowel and uses her small gloved hand to measure the space between pansies. Very neat. Takes a white tea towel and embroiders on a prawn. Rickrack braid along the bottom of her daughter's dress. Years pass. The world is full of places to put her hands.

Then one day, her father goes into a butcher's shop and calmly places his palm below his throat. Tiny twinge before the attack. He moves the hand down over his heart, gasps and falls, smashing his cheek into the whiteness of the floor. This is how it happened, Eleanor's sister tells her. Her voice wobbly on the phone. And soon after this, Eleanor has an affair with a dentist. Drills and mirrors. Cold. The taste of synthetic mint. She lies beneath him as he shines a light into her mouth. *How close he is*, she thinks, *I could look right up his nostrils*, before she notices the clarity of his skin. There is a single ingrown hair in his beard and she wants to reach up and squeeze it out. When she is levered back to sitting, he says she will have to return several times, that there are tiny holes hidden *in that lovely smile*. It is 1974. Eleanor is forty-six. That night as she makes dinner, she notices the reflection of her mouth: a pink streak warped by the curve of the kettle. The shape changes as she smiles. There is a series of appointments. He says, *Call me Jim*, and slides a needle into her gum. She finds herself requesting the last slot in the day.

Eventually, he drives her home and kisses her, her mouth still puffy, tingling, the nerves returning to life. The affair springs quickly into being. It feels miraculous to find love, or at the very least the ability to be entirely fascinated by another person, still lingering in her, intact. The quick of it. Her body floods back to her. The flesh of her stomach and the taste of his gloves. Sliding her tongue over her teeth. She likes his hands as they were when he first explored her mouth. Definite. Firm. They know what they want, and it is her. He wears a dark blue coat and looks like Henry. It is short lived.

Edward says, 'I think I should tell you that I know.'

She wonders how he discovered it. Doesn't ask. Wonders if he has been told. Does not realise that he simply recognises this type of secret – her face animated with private expressions, a small difference in her bearing. He can hear her saying a name inside her head, forming its beautiful letters. She would like Edward to shout, but he doesn't. She comes in and finds him standing with his face in the living-room curtain and thinks he is weeping into the rippling birds. Guilt and love stream out of her. But when he turns, his face is blank. Beyond blank. A field of snow. Tears on her face as he walks out past her. She takes a train to her sister at the seaside.

'There are millions of men in the world,' her sister says, 'millions of men, including your husband.'

Eleanor's voice hoarse over the pebbles. 'I only want Jim.'

Edward picks her up in the car. Doesn't mention it. Tiny rocks in the driveway. Pebbledash on one side of the house. Back to real life. Back to slow. Slow, slow, quick, quick, slow – that was how things seemed to roll out. The house is always messier than she wants. But things are actually easier after the affair. She has broken the binary perhaps, between Henry and Edward. The children ask why they have to go to a different dentist. Comforting them through the death of the first dog. Bringing home another. *See, things can be exchanged if not replaced.*

Edward

1976

Edward's daughter fell in love. He watched her as her being altered. She moved through the house smiling to herself, brutally embarrassed if anyone asked why. Then she gazed out of their kitchen window, returning to it like a dog in the hour before he – the boyfriend – arrived, singing as he walked up the drive, so easy in his body and in Edward's house, a big smile and subtle patina of eczema on his eyelids and wrists. How did people emerge into the world with such confidence? Edward marvelled.

For months, Ruth shone, her mouth raw from his stubble. Men were supposed to hate their daughter's boyfriends. Wasn't that right? But Edward was so amazed by Ruth, her hair cut short in little flicks around her face, reading on a rug in the garden, lying on her belly in cut-off shorts, the sun pinking the backs of her legs. He could not dislike the boy beside her. When a ladybird began to stroll up the ridge of her palm, she called to Edward where he stood in the greenhouse, removing tomatoes from their stalks with a twist of his hand, to share her new delight with the world, *Dad, look at this*. He felt proud of her. It was not because of the boy, who over time struck him as a little gormless.

It was that she could step so cleanly into happiness, that she felt she deserved it. Or perhaps more than that, that happiness was not a thing to be deserved or otherwise. It was a place you could open the gate of and stroll into.

And then one day, when the house was so quiet he thought it was empty, Edward crossed the landing and saw her through the open door of her bedroom, sitting on her bed, her eyes open but passive, her arms hanging strangely at her sides. All her shine had come off. He stopped and she slowly turned her head to look at him, her expression unchanged.

'What is it?' he asked, though he immediately knew.

Twice in his life, Edward had witnessed road accidents, and his daughter had the strange look of a person who had been driving along in one direction and then suddenly found themselves unbuckling their seatbelt and climbing out of something wrecked, a burn mark on the road, the car absorbed by nettles or the newsagent's window all splintered.

'I split up with Geoff,' she said, and burst into tears.

Edward took her out in the car and found himself talking much more than he usually did. It was late summer, the lanes narrowed by thickened hedges. He told her about the summer at the hinge of his childhood, the hottest of his life. He remembered flying a friend's yellow kite, though come to think of it, he could not remember any breeze, just close, sticky air, fruit rotting on the branches before it could be picked. Then his memory turned to the row of newborn labradors, tiny and piglike, born under the table that summer in his friend's kitchen, their blunt faces and closed eyes.

Ruth sat limp in the passenger seat, sweating slightly in her synthetic dress. It was patterned with a print of white daisies. There was spot on her chin, enraged by picking. Suddenly she laughed.

'Dad,' she said, 'why are you telling me all this?'

And he said he didn't know and laughed with her, then pulled into a car park and asked if she was all right.

'Oh, Dad,' she said, and cried fat tears like a little child. 'Oh, Dad.'

He remembered how she used to vomit on long car journeys when she was younger and so for a time was permitted to take her mother's seat in the front. She would fling the door open as soon as he could stop for her, thrust her head out and throw up violently onto the road, her brother, Eddie, holding his nose in the back. The heat of her always shocked him on those occasions as he placed his palm on her heaving back, feeling her little spine moving beneath his hand. Edward wasn't sure now what to say, so he took his cue from the past. He placed a hand on her shoulder and said, 'Yes, that's it, Ruth – better out than in.'

Months later, when she had returned to herself, the boy forgotten fully, Edward found himself staggered by the impermanence of this pain. How the intensity dissipated. He had not known it could be like that. It was as if she had sent all the feeling out from herself and it had dissolved upon contact with the world.

Eleanor

1975–1987

The loosening of Eleanor's body. Her skin a little bigger than her bones. Pin a dart in a borrowed dress. Liver spots and a few stains on the teeth. Eleanor, in a cotton blouse and a cornflower cardigan, feeling the cold with her arms crossed over her chest. White coffee. Her mother dies, after a brief, distressing period of madness. Roses in a glass. Eleanor takes up tapestry. Bright, thick threads. Ruth then Eddie leave home for university. Pride. A glance between her and Edward of *We have done this*. She puts her stockinged feet up on the dashboard as the two of them travel alone.

In 1987, her first grandchild is born. Joseph. Too soon and too small, but he lives. He is so light. The lightest child that has ever been placed in her arms.

Edward

1989

Edward's second grandchild was born. Emily. A girl.

Her arrival in the world was heralded by the telephone, ringing through the house, too early to be anything else. Edward and Eleanor were taking care of Joe. How tiny he was, sleeping, in his mother's old bed. Edward placed a hand upon his back. Joe blinked awake. Sticky eyes and static making a cloud of his hair.

Eleanor

1990–2002

One day, Eleanor stands in the supermarket and sees Henry. Except it isn't him, because this man can't be more than thirty-five. He undoes his dark coat and it's gone. The clothes are wrong. Eleanor is sixty-two. She stands there with a bag of potatoes and thinks, *I have lived a whole life without you*. Then she wonders if he's dead. She walks up the drive with two shopping bags, the handles distending, plastic warping with the weight of her instant coffee, apples and frozen spinach. As she places them on the brick driveway to get her key, Eleanor hears singing from the garage. She is used to Edward practising in there for choir, just the bass lines of songs, which stop and start and don't make sense without the other voices. But he is on the melody for once. *Bathe me in thy tide; wash me with water flowing from thy side.* The beauty of his voice. She does not want to move. Is he standing still, she wonders, on the other side of the sheet of green metal, singing with his shoulders back? Or is he doing something – fixing her shoe with glue where the suede had separated from the sole, his voice coming from his body as easily as it would from the radio? Wind flutters through the shopping bags.

She tries to open the door very quietly, pausing with her fingers round the handle before she pushes down, but there is a faint unsticking sound as the door pulls away from the frame. The singing stops.

She quarrels with Edward. All over the world they keep up the low-level stream of complaints. In Singapore. In Scarborough – the static caravan they take the grandkids to each summer. But there is gentleness too. Kind silences. Joe and Emily crouch at a rockpool to marvel at crabs. She smiles as Edward meets her eye. He is caught in the beam of her love for them.

Her body is old but still contained. She has stayed slim and takes a silly shred of pride in that. It takes some of the sting off when people tell her she must have been beautiful *once*. Aged seventy, she stands at the base of a pyramid. Heels cracked in her sandals. Light-coloured trousers and loose shirt. *Like Anne of the Indies*, she thinks. Her stomach is flat beneath her belt. But her body has begun to fail her. A hollowing in her chest. A falling inward. Pains. Halfway up the steps, she stops, struggling for breath. She tells Edward to go up ahead.

'Is it worth it?' she asks a woman coming down.

The woman smiles, big white teeth in the sunshine. 'No,' she says, in an American accent, 'but you've got to go.'

Final years. Folded nightdress on the pillow. Someone who folds in on themselves a bit. Folds something up, then irons the folds into deep grooves. Who always keeps their gloves in their left pocket, who turns their socks a certain way, so the pattern will show in the ball. Who keeps a house. Keeps.

Maintains. Someone with collectable plates and souvenir spoons. Someone who doesn't know her tastes are slightly crass. Who would be mortified to know. Who hums songs from Gilbert and Sullivan. Directs amateur pantomimes. Someone who thought her life might involve a famous person. Someone who sat in the cinema when she was young thinking, *Perhaps, perhaps.* Someone good at wanting. The kind of wanting that is dangerous. Slightly brittle. Bone china. Who remembers how it felt to dance. Bickering with Edward, forgetting he once felt like new air. Shaking dust out of the hoover. Keeping her eggs in the fridge.

Edward shames her into eating as she begins to die. She takes a year over it. Her, in the pale green chair with a potato on her lap. Her, in the hospital, shrinking under the sheets. Edward brings her a dressing gown, a cardigan. He cares for her body as it fails. Tells her he is recording her soap operas on cassettes. Stands beside her when they draw out blood, until the time he faints, crashing down, caught in a nurse's arms before he gets to the floor. Old now. Maroon pullover. She watches him from the island of her bed. He sits in the chair. They giggle about it, the colour returning slowly to his face. Then he reaches for her hand. A cannula at her elbow crease. He doesn't say, *I love you.* But he does. We have to believe he does. The children and grandchildren come and go. Old people – Eleanor's baby brothers and sisters. They seem far away. But every day there is Edward. She lurches toward death in a morphine dream. Hallucinates that there are white rats in a cage at the end of her bed. Then the feeling of movement as she grows stiller. Feeling of being thrown and caught. Thrown and caught. Thrown

Part Four

Joe & Emily

2012

A letter arrived at our parents' house.

I was standing in the supermarket when my phone rang. The only thing in my basket was a bag of red apples. I slid the basket's handles into the crease of my elbow as I took my phone from my pocket.

'Hi, Emily,' Dad said.

I said, 'Hi, Dad.'

I crossed the aisle to the bags of spinach. I still expected an ordinary thing.

He said, 'A letter arrived for Joe.'

I put the basket down and picked up a bag. The edges of the leaves inside were turning yellow. I put the bag down and inspected another.

'I thought I should call you because they said . . .' Dad paused. He must have the letter in his hand.

I put down the spinach. The crinkle sound of plastic on plastic.

'. . . he can still have treatment, but from now on the emphasis is palliative.'

I stood there very still. A child ran round the corner. A

little Orthodox boy with ringlets resting on the sides of his face.

'Right,' I said.

'I knew you would want to know,' Dad said.

'Yeah. Thank you,' I said.

I looked down at the apples.

'How's Joe?'

'He's upset,' Dad said.

Upset. All the things a phrase can cover. Like, *I'm fine* – all the times that it isn't enough, but also isn't a lie. *I am fine. I am living. When my shower runs cold, I can see all the veins in my chest afterwards, shining through me, fanned out like a tree. My body is working. I am fine.*

'Are you OK, Dad?' I said.

'I am all right,' he said. 'Are you?'

'I'm fine,' I said. 'Is Joe there?'

'He went out.'

'Is he OK?'

'I think he's OK,' Dad said.

OK as in *not unsafe*. *Not unsafe* as in *not about to harm himself*.

'I'm sure he'd like to see you,' Dad said.

'OK, I'll call him,' I said.

Then Dad said, 'I love you.'

And I said, 'I love you.'

My mobile phone was warm. It had recently begun to overheat and turn itself off and I sometimes put it in the fridge – white rectangle on a white plate – to try and cool it down. Now, I pressed it between my palms and willed it to keep working. There was a dent in the casing, silver shining through the white, where I had dropped it on the kitchen tiles. I had been told so many seismic things through this small device. Several months from this moment, the phone would be stolen. A man pretending to be drunk would stand too close to me on the bus and slip it from my pocket and a replacement would arrive in a box with a peel-off sheet of clear plastic to protect its face.

I put the apples away and discarded my basket by the door. Outside, I called you. You were on the train when you answered. I asked where you were going.

'I don't know,' you said. 'I just needed to get out.'

Just a small flutter of panic through your voice.

I told you to meet me and you said, 'OK.'

You said it again after each of my instructions.

'Change at Clapham Junction.'

'OK.'

'Go to platform ten.'

I said you would know you were on the right train if it smelled of burning toast.

'It's a mystery,' I said. 'All the Waterloo trains smell like toast.'

Then I got on the 243 and moved toward you. I was on a backward-facing seat, which made me feel sick. It was hot, though the world outside was cold, but it seemed too crowded to try and get my coat off. Opposite me, a woman sat with a little girl who was holding a sheet of paper with pasta bows and glitter glued onto it.

'Later we can show Mummy,' the woman said.

Her accent sounded Polish, perhaps.

'Mummy will like that,' she said.

How kind of her, or how professional, to keep conjuring up this person who was not there. She placed a tissue over her hand and the child placed her nose in it and blew.

I pictured this woman later. How she would leave the girl and return to her flat to Skype her own mum. Would slip into her own language and say work was fine, the child was fine – sweet really. She wouldn't talk about the man she had been dating, kind and skinny, who made her laugh and smelled like yeast when he made love to her. How she had called it off a few weeks ago but had gone round to his flat last night and accepted a joint, which had flooded her body and immobilised her. There was nothing for it but to lie down giggling on his bed. She'd let him hold her. They had kept their clothes on and he'd only kissed her a few times, on the scalp, because now they were just friends. *Don't love me*, she had told him. He'd said, *Baby, I'll try.* Imagining her life made me feel clean.

The bus kept halting. Suddenly I couldn't breathe. I began to sob. I could hold in the sound but nothing else. Tears fell down my face. My face felt very hot. I pushed my lips hard together. Felt them turning white. When I opened them slightly, breath broke through with a *fffff* sound. I breathed rapidly into my palm. My nose streamed. My eyes streamed. I couldn't stop. And the woman, the nanny, leaned toward me. She gave me one of the child's tissues. Her eyes widened.

'It's all right,' she said. 'It's all right. It's all right.'

She said it over and over again. Weight of my tongue. The deep root of it where the mouth becomes the throat. I couldn't speak to her, but I could hear her through the wall of myself. She had perfume on. I nodded. I felt drugged. I gulped in some air but couldn't say, *Thank you*, as I got off the bus.

On the street, I balled my fists inside my sleeves and dragged them over my face. I let the autumn air cool my skin. I could not let you see me so afraid. I breathed slowly, deliberately. Then I ran my index knuckles gently beneath my eyes. Already dry. I crossed the road and found you downstairs in the station, waiting, as we had agreed, outside McDonald's.

We went into a Lebanese restaurant. It was too cold to be outside. It had a metal floor and high booths nested in scaffolding, which you had to climb up ladders to get to. We climbed up and sat on the bench, on the same side, your coat between us. You said there was still a possibility and I said I believed in it.

Then a waitress popped up her head. Clear skin and a green streak through her hair.

She beamed and said, 'How are you?'

And we both said, 'Fine, thanks.'

We laughed and laughed when she disappeared down the ladder. As if *How are you?* was the best joke we had ever heard. The food arrived. You ate almost nothing, delicately chewing a strip of white cheese. We kept laughing.

You asked Dad to take your portrait. The two of you went out to a pond by our parents' house. The place was optimistically called *The Meadow* on the orange sign by the gate. A concrete path wrapped the pond. Reeds grew round it. It had a modest beauty. One winter, the water froze and I saw a fox trot down the length of it, leaving pawprints in the powdery snow that covered the ice. One bend of the path revealed a willow, bathed, at certain times of day, in golden light. But there were also beer cans in the grass and an overturned shopping trolley at the lip of the water. We used to joke that it was where we would dump a body. Near the entrance, a pair of white trainers dangled by their laces from a tree. You were slow to get ready. Dad did not want to rush you, though he knew he was losing the light. You were in pain. The short walk from the house, down the alley, through the train station and across one road took you almost twenty minutes.

In the image, your hands are in your pockets. Your eyebrows peak up slightly, beneath your hat. A question in your eyes. Tension in the set of your mouth. It is an imperfect photograph. It was too dark. Dad had to use flash, highlighting how yellow your skin and eyeballs had become. You wanted a portrait, a beautiful picture of you. But when it came to it, you could not look at him.

The last time you came to my flat, it was the end of October. It was cold. We went to the pub across the road, owned by two Turkish brothers. I fished the ice out of your juice with a teaspoon. I brought a chessboard out of my bag and the lunchbox containing the pieces. You smiled and I felt like a magician. Apple inside an orange. But I messed up the time of the last train to Seven Sisters and you had one of your contained panics.

'Fuck, fuck,' you said as I put you on the bus to Finsbury Park.

'Joe, it's easy,' I told you. 'It takes the same amount of time. It's just another way to get on the Victoria line.'

But you were tired and ill, and I had failed you. And you never came over again.

I used to cringe when friends said, *Love you, bye*, on the phone to their parents or boyfriends. It seemed like a tic. Always the same tone and rhythm to it. *Love you, bye*. Once, Harriet accidentally included it in a voicemail to her hairdresser. It tumbled from her mouth as she went to hang up.

I asked why her family did it and she shrugged. 'In case something happens.'

Our family had never gone for that kind of prophylactic hurling of *I love you* at each other, but in the last eleven months of your life, we learned to say it often. To state the fact of it.

I love you, Joe.

I know, Emily. I love you too.

One evening, when you were still at home but much closer to death than I realised, you looked up and said, 'I am never going to have a relationship.'

Pain in your body. Your voice tight. You sat at the kitchen table with your hands resting on it, loosely clasped. Circular burns in the wood. Some side effect had made your legs itchy. You scratched them. I sat across from you, cutting cucumbers and mixing them into yoghurt.

I said, 'Joe, you don't know that.'

Dad stood at the stove, making curry. You would usually be helping – cutting onions or laying the table, putting water into a jug and placing glasses by our plates – but you wouldn't be eating much. Besides, there was no strength in your hands.

'It is a central part of life,' you said, agitated.

It was only last Christmas that you had waited until the small hours of the morning to sit opposite me and say you liked someone. Your voice quiet. Your eyes flicking away from me to the window. You were sad, but there was a glimmer of a joke in it. The thrill of sharing a secret.

When your cancer was discovered, you said, 'Well, it's a bad chat-up line.' Your palms open, ironic-exasperated. But you also asked the doctor whether people's partners left at times like this and relayed his response: *It depends.* I picture his shrug, a little question about you passing through his brain before his eyes travelled back to your notes. Once, in a waiting room with Mum, you picked up a green-and-white leaflet about sex after colostomy and rage spread through your body as you read. *Fuck*, you said loudly. *They think I am sixty and have a wife.* Then you asked if she had a pen and wrote, *Heteronormative bullshit*, on the front and slid it back into the rack.

I took a bunch of mint leaves and tore them into the

yoghurt. The smell of curry filled the room and oil rose from the pan and stuck to the walls.

You said, 'I thought I had all this time.'

I got up and turned on the extractor fan behind the microwave. Dad grated a lump of turmeric into the rice, staining the metal and his fingers orange.

He said, 'Our culture centralises romantic love. It's very reductive.'

Your skin was jaundice yellow, your eyeballs yellow like a reptile's.

You said, 'Yeah.'

Later that night, I turned off the television and sat beside you on the sofa.

'I just . . .' you said, hesitating, 'I just liked the idea of being part of an old couple, you know?'

Our grandparents flashed into my mind, sitting together on the beach in Scarborough. Her in her black swimming costume, a raised purple vein snaking up toward her knee, my childish desire to touch that vein, to lay a sheet of paper over her leg and rub it with a crayon until its shape shone through, as she once had shown us how to do on a sheet of etched brass. Him with white hairs on his chest. The two of them bickering as he unwrapped the greasy paper and she pursed her lips and blew to cool our chips.

I said, 'Joe, you know that we all love you, don't you,' answering a question you had not asked.

'Yeah,' you said, 'I know.'

But you wanted another sort of love. The type where another person chooses you and you choose them. You wanted someone to notice you and a little tug to develop inside them, urging them toward you. A mirror tug in you. You had seen it. People luminous around each other. That hungry way of listening, one person's knee slipping between the other person's knees, braced there. You wanted to be beautiful to someone. You wanted your skin touched, not by investigative fingers in surgical gloves – *Does this hurt? What about this?* Hands that chose you. That followed the lines of your body and cared for it as it failed. A healthy hand in your yellow hand. Someone to sit on the ward with you, making jokes with dread blooming in their stomach. Someone who kissed you on the mouth when the nurse wasn't looking.

I had chosen you the least of everyone in your life.

I think of you before you were born. A little unplanned baby, nested inside our mother's body as she travelled around Mexico. Her choice to keep you there. A cluster of cells. Elongating into a tiny cashew nut, the shape becoming human. Your presence making her vomit on dusty buses, making her crave just the whites of hard-boiled eggs. Dad, beside her, eating the yolks from her plate. Their choice before that, to marry each other, to be the beginning of a new family.

Later, she said to him, *Let's have another one.*

And they did, and it was me.

The words around your birth are *accident* and *miracle*. And this is my word: *another*. I never chose you. You were a fact of the world as I found it.

You had some glimmers. You met a man on the train once. Older. You told me about him. You were on your way back to visit our home town. You kissed in the empty carriage. Hills and farms around you, covered by night. You were going to go home with him, but he said, *God, you're so young. You're so young.* You were discovering that you were attractive. Tentatively deploying that small power in the world. There is a photograph of you from the year before you died. Your graduation concert. Your violin shining. Your face open, confident. Something is clicking into place for you. You are handsome in your white shirt. Ready to begin.

November came. You began to feed the robins in our parents' yard. They curled their tiny feet round the washing line and you left pieces of bread for them on the ground. You were weakening. Letters arrived from friends and relatives and people Mum and Dad knew but you and I only loosely remembered.

'You know Julie,' Mum said. 'She took us to Chester Zoo when you were seven.'

People wrote that they remembered you as a boy. Such a clever little boy.

'But that's not who I am,' you said. 'It's like nothing I have done since then counts for shit.'

I told you, 'They don't mean that, Joe,' that people were trying to say that you had left a mark in their memory, that they loved you and felt a connection with you even if they hadn't seen you for a while.

We went to buy bird seed at a pet shop and were greeted at the door by a blue-and-yellow parrot.

'Hello,' I said, and jumped when it said, 'Hello,' in reply.

You coaxed the robins closer to the house, sprinkling seed through your fingers on the back step. We left them scraps of rice and biscuit crumbs. One day, Mum put down the remains of a lemon meringue pie and screamed when she opened the door later to find a rat sitting in the centre of the foil tray. It didn't even run, just sat there gleeful with meringue round its mouth.

You fed the robins but began to dismiss food. Your doctor had said you would be less and less interested in it. You would spend more and more time in bed. Had you asked him outright what dying was? All your tastes changed. No more coffee. You didn't like it anymore. I kept buying you chocolate. Little bears in suits of golden foil.

'Thank you,' you said, and stood them in a row in your room beside your jade animals.

The last time I came over to see you, you told me to be very quiet and opened the back door. A corridor of light came in over the tiles. Your arms had become thin. Above your left elbow, a PICC line was held in place with a white bandage, a dressing over the place the tube went into your vein. You broke a cracker in half and put the pieces on the floor, one by the door and the other in front of the table.

'Wait,' you whispered, your eyes alight.

When the robin hopped in, you looked at me and burst into a smile.

A woman outside university gave me a card offering *Free haircuts with trainee stylist at a top London salon*. It was something to do. I made an appointment for 12 November. When I went, the receptionist was a boy from our home town. He was so fine-featured that everyone had called him Girlface. Seven years ago, he came to a party at our house and slept between me and Harriet in my bed. I had quite liked him and had to slip out to sleep alone on the bathroom floor when I heard the two of them kissing in the night.

He said he lived in London now and smiled ear to ear, proud.

Then he said, 'Listen, is Joe all right?' and said that he'd picked up that maybe you were ill or something from the way people were writing on your Facebook.

'He's got cancer,' I said, a shock of guilt grabbing my throat.

You had just gone into hospital for some procedure: an attempt to strengthen you for further treatment. You were supposed to be in for five days, but it had been seven.

I just said, 'He's having a hard time.'

The boy from home said, 'Wow. Fuck.'

I went downstairs and the trainee stylist cut my hair. Her tutor kept coming over and checking her progress. He picked up some strands at the back of my head and measured them with a ruler. The trainee asked if I would stay for her exam, and when I said yes, she beamed and another woman came over and put make-up on my face, curling my eyelashes tightly round a tiny round brush. I knew I must not cry after that, even when I was ejected into Covent Garden to kill an hour alone. I would ruin the make-up artist's work. I walked round the shops, letting my eyes move from object to object. No one minds when you do that. No one notices and comes up and says, *You have been staring at these boxes of tissues, these apples, these packets of patterned tights for six whole minutes now.* You can fill a lot of time just looking at things.

I returned to parade up and down the little room with my graduated bob, then stood in a line with the other models chosen by virtue of needing a free haircut.

'It looks really good,' you said the next day when I saw you in hospital.

You had gone into hospital for ever, but I did not know.

I remember us hiding together in long grass. I don't know if you would recall it, but in my mind the moment is very clear. Except I don't know when or where it happened. We had not planned to hide, just sat down, unnoticed, on a walk with our parents and realised that the grass rose high above us on all sides. We felt like we had created something, even though we had just found it. When we heard them calling, we wordlessly decided to hold on to our power a little longer and not come out, the light filtering greenly through the grass, even as we heard the panic in their voices mount.

It was late November. Someone had taped tinsel to the reception desk at the hospital. Almost back to Christmas. Our parents were thin. They had been hollowed by the year: months of Mum buttering toast and getting cheese out and cutting cake up on a plate, putting it down in the living room with a huge terrified smile but never eating any. Of Dad's cheeks seeming to fall out of his face. But we can't all shrink. Someone needs to lift the bodies out of the bed.

I sat with Mum and Uncle Eddie, a white tablecloth over our thighs. He'd come to the hospital with biscuits and grapes and a book of puzzles for you.

'Thank you, thank you,' you told him, your face yellow and voice cracked.

I saw him glance at the bag of fluid from your lung. They had drained out two litres, the doctor said. I thought of the big bottle of flat lemonade in Grandad's car.

'Please,' Uncle Eddie begged Mum, 'you need to eat. Let me take you out.'

This may have been the first time I truly thought about them as siblings. We got into his car and went to a restaurant, while Dad stayed by you reading the newspaper aloud as you drifted asleep and awake. Tannin taste of wine. The place was too posh because he needed so badly to give us something.

We talked and laughed, but then Mum put down her fork and wept, 'My baby, my baby,' until the waiter brought napkins. Waistcoated, embarrassed, plump.

Mum and Dad began staying with you in hospital. Sleeping in the chair beside your bed. Welcoming visitors until you became too tired for that. I came and went. I told you about university, about Solomon's friend who came to our flat and ate a daddy-long-legs. I tried to do both lives, ricocheting toward and away from you on trains and buses and once in Solomon's car. *Conserve your energy, Emily*, everyone said. *He might be there months.*

But they were doubly wrong. It was not months, and it took more energy to come and go than to stay there in the hospital. Sanitiser on my hands on the way in and out. Finding myself back in the normal world where nobody knew what was happening. Travelling through London in the dark, flipping the camera on my phone to use it as a mirror and spreading make-up over my skin. Colour on my eyelids and cheeks. Putting on bracelets and rings and going to the end-of-term party in a student flat. A steely feeling. I hoped to anchor myself to the living world. My naked shoulders in my dress. A bottle of cheap Prosecco. Watching Yusuf getting drunk.

'What have you been doing today, Emily?' Claire said. 'Cool haircut, by the way.'

Not wanting to tell her but not wanting to lie.

'I have been in hospital visiting my brother.'

'He's going to be OK, though, isn't he?'

People kissing on the sofa, their eyes closed as if no one else was there. Laughter. Somewhere, a breaking glass.

'Actually, no,' I said. 'He's not.'

Going into a ticket office for a new Oyster card because mine was lost. The man who smiled and was kind. Wanting to cry because this person must be that gentle and easy with everyone. It wasn't because you were dying. He didn't know anything about that.

'Did he fancy you?' Solomon asked when I tried to explain.

Procedures were scheduled, then cancelled. Once, when I was there, you attempted to get up out of bed to go to the toilet. The effort — of sitting, climbing off the bed and walking to the bathroom trailing your drip, using the toilet and re-emerging to reverse the sequence — left you winded with exhaustion, wincing in pain in the bed. You were very weak. One evening, you weren't allowed to eat and you begged me for a sachet of salt.

'He's been talking about seeing Grandma,' Mum said.

I thought of you and me with our arms crossed over our chests when everyone else at school got up for communion, the only pupils unconfirmed and unbaptised. You had always been so rational and now you were making appointments with the dead.

'Really?' I said.

'He said he wants to see Grandma and Helga.'

Helga had died one Christmas when you forgot to put away a box of Quality Street. She snuck into the living room and ate them all. It made her stomach twist inside her and she died of torsion. Our dog who was secretly luminous beneath her black fur.

I saw you receive a blood transfusion. It amazed me, the blood arriving and being strung up next you, the colour rising in your face as the bag emptied into your veins. Strong, clean blood.

'Better than a double espresso,' you joked.

Once I was there and a doctor, who couldn't have been more than a few years older than you, pulled back the curtain round your bed but did not step in. He wanted to quickly get your permission not to be resuscitated before he went off shift.

It was a Thursday night. Early December. I was in my bedroom, hanging out my towel and swimming costume to dry, making sure they hung flat between the radiator and the wall. Mum called.

'Hi, love,' she said.

'How is he?' I said.

I had not turned on the light. I sat down beneath the window to listen, the wet things against my back. The orange streetlight shone in. Its glow touched my shoulders. I had made an extra bookshelf on top of the dresser with planks of wood and food tins. Inside were potatoes, their pale bodies preserved like the pickled calf foetus in a jar at our school, with its soft face, like it could wake up anytime. *I like your shelf,* you had said when you saw it. *Provisions for the apocalypse.*

I thought Mum might say that you were coming home.

She took a breath, then told me, 'He's moving to the hospice this weekend.'

Next door, Solomon was watching an episode of *The Simpsons.* I felt not calm but slow. My heart was not racing. It was an episode I had seen before, so I could almost see the images as the voices came through the wall.

So here we were in winter. The roads tight with frost.

Memory of eating the glittering grit laid out in our infant-school playground.

Memory of a train ride through Austrian mountains, Harriet's feet in my lap. The winter five years before, when I was eighteen, embedded awkwardly into another family. Mum had got a new job in London and the house where we had been raised suddenly needed to be packed up and left. The independence of our parents shocked us. It had never crossed our minds when we left home that they might also do so. You and I came back to deal with our possessions and spend a final Christmas there, but it was already different because the photos had all come down and the walls had been painted Pure Brilliant White.

It looks like a hospital, you said.

When I went back to Austria, our house was sold to strangers, who would make their own stories in it.

I wonder if they lived there more carefully than us, less prone to breaking and burning things. Brush through the little girl's hair before bed, and mint and pink plastic horses lined up on her windowsill. A list of meal plans on the fridge.

I wonder about the couple who moved out before we moved in, leaving so many of their things behind because they had lost interest in their joint life. By now, perhaps they had found ways to be around one another again, to smile and ask each other questions at the wedding of their grown-up son, rather than standing at opposite ends of the room, arms folded over their smart clothes. Perhaps one day, they found themselves on the same bus, bumping over the moor, and realised they were both travelling toward the chemo ward, books and newspapers in their bags and comfortable clothes on, and had laughed at the bleak humour of being drawn back together like that. Perhaps they did, and perhaps they discovered that, in face of life and death, it was in fact possible to be open-faced and kind, but in a different way to how they had been in the past, nothing breathless in it. I wonder if the pair of knickers left in the sofa belonged to the wife or the woman he had an affair with.

Once, a very old man stopped me on the pavement outside that house, pointed at your window and told me he was born in that room. I was fifteen then and just said, *Really?* and went shy and couldn't find any proper questions. Perhaps the man had an older sister who was allowed into that room full of screams. Perhaps the sister found the ordinary violence of it terrifying and made sure she was never ripped up like that. Or maybe she became a midwife because she realised that she could do this, that inside her was some unlearned knowledge of exactly how to be.

A few months later, I sent you a postcard from Austria, describing how I had run round my apartment block during a rainstorm, the way the streets had smelled so fresh as if the rain had lifted something from them. As I put it into the yellow postbox, I realised that we really did not live together anymore. We had grown up.

I came into your room on Friday. We knew you were moving to the hospice, but I did not say, *Joe, I am so sorry that you are dying.*

I said, 'It's good to see you sitting in the chair.'

The room was full of food you didn't want. Treats. Trays of vegetarian sushi. Chocolates, rolls from the hospital friends shop, cut and filled with cheese and sliced cucumber by widows and widowers with papery hands. You said, *Thank you*, to whatever was brought but waved it away. *Maybe later*, you said, but I am not sure you believed it. Three times a day, a smiling Romanian woman came to ask if you wanted a meal. She remembered everybody's names. Sometimes you said yes, but rarely actually ate. Eventually, Dad would take off the sweating plastic lid, pick up your cutlery and swallow the food down cold. He had learned in some previous pocket of life never to waste. All you wanted to do was drink. Dad mixed up orange squash in the kitchen we had discovered in your third week on the ward. He brought it in to you.

'Is it the right strength?' he asked as you drank it through a straw.

Mum bought cartons of pineapple juice from the shop downstairs. Seeing you drink was wonderful, like watching our animals latch on to the metal spouts of the bottles bound to their cage, bubbles rising as they sucked out the water.

Dad took a photograph of us in front of the window. You did not ask him not to. Perhaps you wanted images, records of your being. Perhaps, after a life of being photographed – Dad at the breakfast table asking you or me to hold up a glass, so the refractions of light fell in a certain

way over the wood – it would have felt worse to not capture these moments. Would render your illness obscene.
In the image, my whole body is turned to you. Blue dress,
my neat, blunt haircut, a person from another world. You
slender in your hospital gown. The muscles visible in your
arms, though they too have shrunk. Visible because there
is so little flesh over your bones. Your face yellow, a tube
in your nose. You look down at your hands and I look at
you.

Mum came in with a clear plastic cup of milk.

'What about this?'

A look between her and Dad, like this was something
they had planned. Dad put a straw in it and placed it on
the wheeled table in front of you. Careful. Hopeful. All
their big hopes for you had become so small.

'Maybe later,' you replied.

He tipped it away.

Our parents' clothes were crumpled. Their faces were
crumpled. They had been there for weeks.

'Go home,' I told Mum and Dad. 'I can stay with Joe.'

I went into the hall with them and we talked quickly
in hushed voices. You see this all over hospitals: people
having huddled conversations away from the sick, already
leaving them out of things.

'Are you sure you'll be all right?'

'Yes.'

'We'll be back first thing.'

'I'll be all right.'

'You can call us. We'll keep our phones on all night.'

They so wanted to be the grown-ups still. But I knew

she would collapse onto him as they walked through the car park. That she would weep and weep, and then gather herself and find a steely voice to say, *I am still optimistic.* I knew that he would tell himself that dealing with her was the difficult thing. Would use that to shield out the rest of it.

I told them I would be fine and watched them walk away.

Alone in the room full of machines, we had our first proper conversation in ages. Just the two of us. The place to ourselves. You had been given your own room because it wasn't appropriate for Mum to sleep overnight on the men's ward. There was a window onto the car park and a pinboard opposite your bed with cards on it. Pins through the pictures – a heron, a mountain, a still life with a silver bowl of limes. I sat by your bed in the lamp-lit dark.

'Emily?' you said.

'I'm here.'

'Do you want my violin?' You asked so quietly that I climbed onto the bed to be close enough to hear.

'Do you want it?'

I hesitated and said, 'I'll look after it for you.'

You frowned.

I said, 'Of course I want it. Thank you, Joe.'

Sound of a trolley down the hall. A nurse coming on shift, the chat between him and the one heading out. Coughing from the shared ward. A tap being turned on, then off. The subtle hum of the lights and the louder hum of the machines.

'Joe . . .' I hesitated, 'do you, like, want me to learn to play it?'

You laughed. You touched your side because laughing was painful and said no.

'OK.'

You chuckled and said, 'You're too old.'

I laughed. You closed your eyes for a moment, opened them and asked for water. I filled a plastic cup from the jug on your nightstand. A cold-sweat smell. Your hair had grown long, fluffy all over your head.

'Just a second,' you said, and pulled yourself up a little in the bed.

Effort of that. The action of pressing into your wrists, shifting your bottom back, straightening your spine. I placed another pillow behind you. You breathed heavily. You brought your palm over the muzzle of your face and I understood you wanted the oxygen mask. I reached for it, passed it with the water cup still in my other hand. Clumsy. You held it over your face, breathing.

'Better?' I asked.

You nodded and pulled it off and I put it to the side. Then you asked again for the water and I passed it to you and you drank about a centimetre. Texture of the hospital sheet. How narrow you were under it. Puckering shape to your lips – should I have given you a straw? Elbows tucked in, holding the cup to your face with both hands. Your movements had narrowed too. You passed the cup back to me and I put it down. We sat silently for a while.

Then I said, 'How are you feeling about going into the hospice tomorrow?'

It was the closest thing I could say to *I am sorry you are dying*.

You nodded to yourself, agreeing with something internal.

'I'm ready,' you said.

You had been baptised. Just a few days ago, when you had more voice, you called a friend who had become a priest (how did you know someone like that? Where had you found the confidence to make the call?) and he came down to London on the train, put the holy water in a cardboard hospital container usually used for vomit. Mum had told me on the phone, and Dad had texted me a photo of the bowl. I found myself unsurprised by the revelation that you believed in God.

I slept beside you on the fold-out sofa in the room, pushing it right up next to your bed so that I could hold your hand. In the night you became confused.

'The beds are too close together!' you suddenly cried, and I felt terrible.

Sometimes you mimed eating sandwiches or handing things to people. I giggled at you in the dark. Sometimes your voice was so quiet and far away that I couldn't tell what you were saying.

'We need a spare oxygen mask,' you announced, 'in case this one breaks.'

'I can ask the nurse,' I said.

'They can bring the oxygen. I'll bring the sheeting.'

'What sheeting?'

'To make the masks.'

You wanted to get out of bed and onto a chair, so I got you a chair, but you thought there was a trapdoor beneath it. You did not know where you wanted to be. In bed, on the chair, in the bathroom. You kept pulling at your hospital gown, so I got your pyjamas. You said that you hated pyjamas, so I put them back in the cupboard. You were in pain. I took you to the bathroom and stood outside with the door ajar. You crouched on the floor, your gown hanging off. Your spine and your naked back. I didn't know whether to go in. The sound of your crying was terrible. I called the nurse and stood in the corridor waiting for someone to come. Then I was on the floor with the nurse standing over me. I must have fainted. The sick, rushing feeling of my blood pressure trying to climb back up. I had let you down. I told the nurse to leave me and go in to you. I sat on the floor in the hall as he changed your gown and helped you to sit up again in the chair. I did not leave you alone in the bathroom again. I believe this was the most important night of my life.

You were moved to the hospice, sitting up in a wheelchair as they took you out to the ambulance. Mum travelled with you, and I followed with Dad in the car. *You are very lucky*, we were told because a room for you was available with another room attached to it, with a fridge and kettle and sink, and sofas for the rest of us to sleep on. We could all stay. Dad parked, and we sat together silently for a moment longer than needed. This seemed to have become a small ritual between us, our other stolen moments of quiet, practices for this one, when at last there was nothing to say.

When we entered, you were sitting on the sofa, calm. I think you were happy, in fact. There was to be no more treatment. You were allowed to stop trying to live. Mum took out a punnet of blueberries and rinsed them and we passed them between us. I sat beside you, and Mum and Dad sat on the other sofa. You ate some and how we all smiled. I think we were relieved too. We were allowed to stop pretending the world was any bigger than this.

For a few days you were graceful, between bouts of extreme distress, morphine hallucinations that made you whisper-shout, 'Get back! Please! I am going to explode!'

You repeated it intermittently – *Explode, going to explode* – until you calmed down. Mostly you slept.

And then you received your last visitor. A nurse unhooked you from the wires and closed the cannulas. A button on the bed was pressed to hinge you up to sit. A hard breath and you moved your legs, pivoted so they hung over the side of the bed. You rested. Our father slid a dressing gown over your hospital gown. Everything hurt. He and I sat either side of you, your arms over our shoulders as we slid slippers onto your feet. Sharp ankles. You smelled different now.

'Ready?'

'Ready.'

We stood. We helped you across the room. One of your teachers had arrived and was sitting next door with our mum. The one you had seen the year in with. We could hear the murmur of conversation and a sound that may have been a sob or a laugh. You were exhausted but rabbit-eyed alert. I thought of small creatures with soft throats. Everyone was pretending that taking half an hour to get up and meet a visitor was normal. We shuffled you to the door and left your sides, knowing it was important that you stood alone to go in. You put your hand on the handle, pulled it down, pushed the door and went through. When she saw you, she lit up and crumpled. You walked very slowly to the sofa and sat down beside her. You spoke together about music and she leaned into you because your voice had become so small. You had told me once that you were afraid of her, as if it were a sort of praise. Now here she was, with soft orange hair, telling you that you had been her best-ever student. Was that true? It was true now.

After that, your body shut down and the animals arrived. The hospice was a hoop with a concrete courtyard in the centre and a moat of garden round the edge. Through the window, I watched fat squirrels and a rat. A volunteer went from room to room with a dog and we unquestioningly received the gift of its presence. It started to feel strange that in normal life such things were not offered. One night, I saw a young man walking through the corridors with a budgie on his shoulder, graceful as a dream.

There are no signs to tell you something is the last time. A doctor came who was very different from the hospital doctors. Everything with her was slower and gentler. She could afford to have a different manner because she was not trying to fix you. She explained that to stem the pain, they would begin to use stronger drugs. You would sleep more and more, and then you'd die. But she didn't say, *He has already taken his last shower* (Dad in there with you, you leaning onto him and his clothes getting wet as the water ran over your skin), or, *He has already been to the toilet the for the final time* (your urine a luminous, medicated orange in the bowl. Like nothing I had ever seen). I did not know that our final conversation was already past. There were brief episodes of consciousness, you swimming up to the place we were. Once, you opened your eyes and I spoke to you.

'Hi, Joe. I just wanted to say. Thank you. For the things you shared with me. I am proud that I was the one you told things to.'

I felt so grateful then for the paltry secrets we'd exchanged at our parents' kitchen table in the dark.

Later, I wondered if you'd even heard me, but my dad assured me, 'He did.'

Mum said, 'He definitely did.'

Sometimes you swam up but didn't quite emerge. Little twitches of awareness.

I think your final words may have been, 'I have pissed the bed.'

Visitors and letters came. People sent cards and books and an art kit in which one could scratch along brown lines on black paper with a special pick to reveal a silver tiger underneath. All of it too late. We read the notes to you as your eyelids flickered. Opening the envelopes and unfolding letters. One from Harriet. One from your first ever music teacher. One from Boston.

Some friends of yours turned up. Two girls and a boy who had arrived together on the train. They sat and spoke to me because you couldn't talk anymore. *Who are these people?* I thought, because I had always made the friends, when were younger and lived in the same place. I had always gone out into the world and harvested people and brought them home to share. Now, I took your friends into the art room, a cold conservatory, took coloured sheets of paper from a plastic basket and showed them how to make paper swans. This is what you do. This is how you be in this place. We sat at the trestle table, folding our swans and decorating them with felt-tip pens. A little plug-in heater whirred down by our feet. We talked about you.

One of the girls said she had asked you out over and over again before she had realised you were gay.

'I mean, I thought I was asking him out,' she added. 'I am not completely sure he noticed.'

They said you were funny. Shy. They said that the four of you had made pancakes together on Pancake Day and watched a squirrel that had lost its tail run round your campus.

'Did it look like a rat?' I asked.

'No! It looked like miniature bear.'

I was so proud of you for knowing these kind people. That they were here, unable to go into your room now, but near you, walking out with me in the courtyard. The square, concrete pond had frozen. One by one we placed the paper birds onto the ice.

When you and I were maybe seven and nine, we found a swimming pool that was slowly turning into a pond, its clean lines mossing over, rust on the rails of the steps and the surface of the water blanketed with leaves. You said I would be able to walk over them if I trod lightly. *She could have died*, Mum shouted at you, very cross.

Solomon arrived, bringing me a change of clothes. Jogging bottoms, a T-shirt, a warm jumper and thick, soft socks.

'I thought you'd want to be comfortable,' he said as he handed them over in the car park.

I told him he had done a good job.

I gave him a tour. Reception with its plastic Christmas tree. I made him a tea in the shared sitting room. The corridors with doors onto small wards of ashen, dying people. The art room. The smoking room. The quiet room with candles burning and a maze drawn on the floor.

'It's very calm,' he said.

'Isn't it perfect?' I said. Like we were choosing a place to get married.

I showed him the family room, adjacent to your room, and said, 'We're very lucky to have this.'

When he came into your room, he could not speak.

He had come to hospital just two weeks before and said,

'He looked better than I expected,' as we drove home.

That made me turn my body into the passenger seat and weep. I was so angry that he did not understand at all. Now, he looked at you on the bed, choked and went breathless. Tears all over his face. Then he asked me to tell you something. He couldn't say it to you.

He turned away and said, 'Please tell Joe I am here and I am going to look after you your whole life.'

Late one night, I saw a woman dab a little hand sanitiser on her tongue from the dispenser in the hall. She turned away ashamed when she saw me see her. The comic guilty freeze of a dog who has eaten the defrosting lasagne left on the side.

When I was alone with you, I sang. Our songs from school. Me in the choir and you bowing the swooping descants. I remembered how I had pencil-marked my breaths. *The Lord is my shepherd* – breath – *I shall not want* – breath – *He maketh me* – breath – *to lie down in green pastures* – breath. Your breath was audible and your lips all cracked. You weren't supposed to drink anymore, but we were given a pink sponge on a stick and shown how to dip it into water and run it over your mouth for relief. Dad was very contained, except when he remembered that he had bought you a present but left it at home. A first edition of some printed chamber music. Not quite your thing but close enough. He burst into tears. It was the finality of forgetting it. There would be no opportunity to go back and pick it up until after you were dead.

All our various family came and went. Dad's sisters

– one of them a florist – who slept in her van in the car park. I wondered if her mattress smelled of leaves. Mum's brother, Eddie. Great-aunts and -uncles, who brought with them the uncanny reminder of Grandma's accent. Grandad, looking tired, with a newspaper and a pencil for the crossword. They sat in the family room and I tried to make tea. Couldn't count out the cups. I think I made fifteen and no one wanted any of it. The cups sat all around in clusters going cold. An older cousin arrived in her car and for some reason I felt ferociously angry at her. Because she didn't know you. All she had really seen was the little boy, too sensitive, obsessive, too difficult. And now this weak thing. I wanted to say to her, *That isn't Joe. There is a whole person between those two points that you never, ever knew.* Wanted her to realise that. But you could no longer speak.

I imagined it. I asked Dad if it would be all right, when it happened, to climb up onto the bed and hold you. Yes, he said, he thought it was fine to do that. I couldn't do it yet: there were too many vital tubes to knock out of place. Was the moment going to arrive gently, I wondered, or would it be a shock, a shot to the stomach, the taste of my blood rising up to meet my throat? Why did I think like that, bullets and blood? Mum agreed to be still when it was time, not to scream. She sat beside me on the fold-out sofa in the special family room, nodding at me, little circles of amber on her earlobes. She promised. I rubbed on hand sanitiser, imagined it and waited for the miracle.

So, this was us. This small collection of people. The others sat with cooling cups and Mum and Dad and me going in and out of your room, drawn back around you. You a little fire. Your eyes like mine under the closed lids. I thought of the us that would be there instead if we had formed into a different constellation of accidents.

Random, the geneticist had said.

The word ripped my imagination. What about the web of cause and effect it took to make us? I felt lives thundering through me. *Random* was so beautiful and so violent. I braced my body against the force of it.

I lifted you, up out of bed. I breathed good air into your lungs, only air and no black fluid, and sealed up the holes in your body. I touched your tumour and it shrank back to nothing beneath my hand. Then I led you, backwards out of the room, down the blue corridors, out of the doors, into the car park and the frosty world. I led you back, through our stories and into the stories before ours. A fist folded round a red ring. Shoelaces unknotting and trodden into grass. A woman's face against the shoulder of a man, cattle moaning outside.

Some nurses came in and bathed you with cloths, section by section so that you were never lying naked. It was a rhythmic, beautiful thing. When your abdomen was exposed, I saw the lump shining through you. Your tumour. Yellow like the whites of your eyes. Swollen. Later when they were gone, I asked you if I could look at it again. You couldn't reply. I pulled down your bed covers and gently lifted your gown. So there it was. It was real after all. There was the wound. I told you about my plan, when it happened, to get onto the bed and hold you. Whispered, hoping you could hear.

But I still felt the miracle. The shiver of the miracle nearby.

Mum and I were almost sleeping on the sofas next door when Dad came in and got us up. He knew that it was about to happen, though he did not tell us how he knew and we did not ask.

He just said, 'I think you should come through.'

I put my hand in yours, but you had no grip left. Your breathing had changed. The sweet, stale smells of breath and skin. A look on your face almost like concentration, like you were searching through yourself for the effort to do this final thing.

Dad said steadily, 'Just let the beauty wash over you.'

He said that again and again.

And then you died.

I felt like we were supposed to get a nurse straight away because it felt important to tell them, so the time on the certificate was correct. It was dark outside. I went into the room with candles and walked the maze drawn out on the floor. One foot. Next foot. Rolling them, heel, mid-foot, toe. It was very quiet. Dad came in and stood in the doorway. Then I went back and did what I had told you, climbing onto your bed and wrapping you up. I slid hands behind your shoulder blades. Dad took photographs, my cheek on yours, even though you were dead. It seemed wrong to miss the final opportunity. My hair finer and lighter than yours, hanging very flat over my scalp. Grey-green eyes like your eyes. Thickness of your lashes. Your dead face loosening to reveal a stripe of eye white.

Edward

2012

Edward lay at home in bed, body still but a flickering under his eyelids. He dreamed of nettles – rising in shadow from dark earth, filtering light, the serrated edges of their leaves. A rash spreading over a naked calf and the skin behind a boy's knee. A stream. Downstairs, the telephone rang, screaming into the empty house. After the final ring, he opened his eyes, closed them, turned onto his side. Awareness that he was dreaming. Dream bleeding into the room. He saw an overlay of nettles against the bedroom furniture. As if they had grown through the carpet. Memory of laying an old rug over weeds to kill them. Rolling it up with Eleanor, raking up the dead plants, squashed and white. Worms frantic, shocked by the light. Edward's lips parted and closed. He let out a snore.

When he woke properly, his tongue was dry.

Joe, he thought.

He walked down the hall to the bathroom, placed his hands on the lip of the sink, bent and put his face under the tap. He was a wolf. Green sink, green bath, green tiles where the walls met the ceiling with white tiles underneath. Chosen by Eleanor, put in by him. Smudge of grout. A line not quite straight. The water was cold as he swallowed it. *Lapping like a dog*, Eleanor said to him. But he didn't listen. She had been dead for twelve years.

Tension gripped his legs at the top of the stairs. *Please.* The word pressed against his brain. *Please, please.* He stood still for a moment, gathering the strength to descend. The strength to lift the telephone from its cradle and listen to the messages. Halfway down, he saw a man on the stairs – himself, were he able to lie down and cry. His face in the carpet. Snot into the roses and shoe dirt in his mouth. But Edward did not do that. He never did things like that. There was no one there to get him up again. He reached the bottom step. *Please.* His heart sped. He did not want to look. Through the frosted glass of the living-room door he saw the red light on the telephone flashing. A message. Edward pushed the door open and looked at the big clock on the wall behind the television, its face flanked by carved horses. Dust in the grooves. Thought of snapping a horse off by its thin legs and carrying it in his pocket. Someone had called him before 8 a.m. He took the phone out of its stand and sat in the chair with it. *Please.* He dialled.

Since January, his daughter Ruth had been calling him every week. He would mute *Question Time* and listen. Silent arguing faces on the screen. Talk about Joe. A horrible feeling like a punch in the solar plexus as she spoke. Sometimes brittle-bright – *He's at the cinema. He's got a friend visiting. He's out for the day with Emily.* Sometimes the language of treatment. Ruth talked about the power of each new drug, of surgery. The power of raspberries and turmeric. At first, she said, *It's very hopeful*, and then, *It's still hopeful*, and finally, *I'm still hopeful*. In their last call, he told her, *I know it should be me*, his voice even but coming from the punch, the flat truth of it bursting from the place where his ribs met. Afterwards, he kept the television silent for a while. Looked at the stupid figures on the screen. So emphatic. The way they moved their hands. He didn't want to watch them, but his body seemed stitched to the chair. Sometimes he shouted at them. Sometimes he closed his eyes, pushed them tight like he was shutting everything beyond out. He pressed his lips together to make sure no sound could come from him. Eventually, his face would relax, his body collapsing back. He often woke there hours later. The room cold. The television playing silently in the dark.

The clear female voice said, *Welcome to your BT answerphone. You have two new messages. First new message.* His son-in-law's voice. *Please, please*, Edward thought for a second. Then the *please* dropped out of him. Left a hollow place where it had been living. Joe was dead. Edward pressed *3* to save the message, though he would never listen to it again. Then he listened to the next message, which was from his son, Joe's uncle. *Dad*, it began. No *hello*, just *Dad*. He said he would be there to pick Edward up at 9.30. Blankness spread through him. A high, white, ringing sound.

The year had been like a pregnancy. Diagnosis to death. Seed of something, growth, fruition. Memory of Eleanor's pregnant body in bed, her weight different beside him as each baby grew. Curve of her back in her nightdress with the pale clinging material catching the light from the clock. He remembered how the same small shoulders, lumbar curve and knees tucked up toward the chest had looked different after he discovered her affair. How it felt to lie close to her, *knowing*, his spine braced against the sheets, eyes open in the dark. Eleanor would be better at this than him. She would go to the hospice and open her arms to their daughter. Cry with her but then wipe the tears away and fiercely grip her hand. When Edward's father died, he had come in with his coat on and she had slid her arms round him. Her narrow shoulders, the bones of her elbows and hips. Her small wrists. If she was alive today, she would stride into the place, open-faced. Available. But it would also squash her. He saw her on their bed, a fist in her mouth. Body convulsing. Sobs. And he was grateful that she didn't know anything about it. Edward would not sob. He knew that. Edward was very good at pulling himself in and moving forward.

He drew a bath, stood still on the landing as it ran. Thunder of the water. Graduation photographs on the wall. He took off his pyjamas, sat on the edge of the bathtub and placed his feet into the water. Like dangling your legs into a stream except the water burned. He turned on the cold tap and felt cold water blooming through the hot. Then he placed his hands on the sides of the bath and lowered down into it. Joe's body lay elsewhere cooling. Edward looked at his flesh. Skinny with loose pouches of fat on the chest, the stomach, the white hair on his legs. He lifted his arms and examined his dry, pink elbows, the tiny vaccination scar on his left arm. Miraculous, really, the way a body is made. The way it articulates. An acute feeling of love rushed at him and crashed over his body. Love for Joe. For all his family. Memory of standing waist-deep in the sea in Scarborough. Holding Joe round his middle as a small boy so he could practise kicking his legs in the water. Emily splashing nearby, but Joe so cautious – *Don't let go of me, Grandad.*

Edward breathed in and sank down to submerge his face.

A memory, quick and slight – Joe cartwheeling in the garden. Then a memory of himself as a teenager. His young body. And then two boys, their eyes on each other, surrounded by stinging nettles, holding their breaths. Memory comes nested in memory. In the shard of one thing, the reflection of something else. Or does that only happen when you take part of your life and snap it into small pieces? Small and sharp-edged so you never have to look at all of it at once. Edward opened his eyes. He saw the surface of the water above him, the ring of green tiles, the ceiling.

Snake backwards through time and find him somewhere else. Find him in the hidden place he had to climb through a hedge to reach. The slip of dirty stream. The factory. The path. Edward in his young skin before he knew the end of this story. Before he left home and learned to be a teacher. Such a different life from his mum and dad's. An indoor existence. Books and radiators, chalk instead of stone. Before he met Eleanor, a Busby Berkeley angel a little older than him. She seemed brave to him. Her small body determined in the blue of the swimming pool. He married her and only sometimes thought about Jack. Bubbles of memory rising to the surface. A pencil-slim boy. Meeting him – *People say your house is haunted.* Two lads sat too close together at school, naked knees touching under the desk. Getting older together and something unspoken but known emerging between them. Finding reasons to touch one another – *There is a fly on your cheek, Ed. Lint on your shirt, Jack*, brushing it away with flat fingers, skin under the fabric, the slim band of muscle, ribs, blood moving urgent and thick round the heart.

When Eleanor betrayed him, Edward thought, *We can all have affairs, you know. We could all choose a different life.* Except he could not. He did not know how to begin. There were moments, over the years, but nothing really. A few looks that lasted too long. Not knowing how to make more of it. Edward and his wife spent their last few decades together on the watch, flashing little insults, the glint of metal, litany of complaints. As if to say, *You have shown me your knife, but look at my weapons. I can hurt back.*

After her death, he thought about Eleanor in the garage mostly, the one part of the house she had barely gone into. He took her glasses out of her handbag, rattling inside their case, and placed them on the shelf above his tools. He felt held in there, by the rough, wide paintbrushes, by all the accumulated things that had a feel and a smell and a purpose, saved scraps waiting for use, the ball of red elastic bands dropped by the postman, oils – for the car, for hinges, for treating wood. In the house, every room felt both empty and too full, with too many plates and too many metres of carpet, possessions that had never belonged to him at all. The garage was where he had gone when the children decided they didn't like hearing the bass line of everything, standing among the tins of paint to practise 'Gentlemen of Japan' and those first low whispers of *Requiem, Requiem.* He took her tapestry frame in there and did his best to weave in the final threads. Surrounded by parts of things saved up for another day, he thought of the conversations they had never had, words that might once have had a moment to be spoken in a quiet evening with the television off, not just muted, their hands round cups and cars sliding quietly past outside, briefly spilling light across the room. He took her glasses back into the house. He had wondered then if a day would come when he didn't think of Eleanor. But it did not. There was no beginning to remembering her, no end. He would realise, in the supermarket, that he had been conducting a conversation with her in his mind for an hour. He kept her glasses by the bed and lived in the endless loop of her.

Soon he would have to dress. Shirt, tie, brown trousers, V-necked jumper, jacket, beige coat. The uniform of his life. His son, Eddie, would arrive at the door with tears on his face. They would get into the car. Fear in them. The knowledge that there was no way to fix the thing that they were moving toward. But love – and something beyond it, the web between people, pulling them forward, carrying them to Joe. Edward, on the motorway in the passenger's seat. A packet of iced buns on his lap. The heating on. Sliding into the hospice car park. His grand-daughter's boyfriend meeting them at the door. Hugs between people who did not normally hug. Going inside. Hugging his daughter. All her fat gone and no colour in her face. Going into the room Joe had died in, knowing he was about to see the body. Seeing the body. The body. Mid-morning in the room. Water on the window. A blind hanging down over it in long stripes. Clutter of a life round the bed. Cards. A folded jumper. Stillness. Making himself look.

Then a ripping feeling as he opened his mouth to say, 'Joe, it's Grandad.'

A few years ago, Ruth told him Joe had come out. Ease of the phrase.

So, Joe came out, she said, as they waited with Mark for their meal to arrive in a restaurant.

He pulled up out of the bath water, felt the wave his body made as the surface broke. Joe. His life stopped. Edward thought of his grandson's purposeful fingers, the way he'd practised every day, even in the holidays when the kids had been delivered to him and Eleanor, the same few scales echoing up the stairs or filling the caravan. Edward had never worked out where to put his hands. Eleanor had missed Joe growing up, playing difficult music, shining as he walked onto the stage. She would have loved the glamour, the feeling that this special person belonged to her. But now he was grateful that she had missed all of that because she was missing this too. Those hands on hospital sheets. Edward had moved through his own life so hesitantly, always wondering when someone was going to ask what he was hiding, but no one ever had. He had hidden too well. Taken a part of himself and put it away as if it were dead. How arbitrary it seemed now. Random that he had ever lived at all.

Edward breathed out.

Part Five

Emily

2012

You died aged twenty-five years, nine months and four days.

I closed the door on your body. Twice, I opened it again, as if I would catch you rolling onto your side and getting up.

I kneeled in the adjacent room and cleared the fridge for the next family. I accidentally spilled blueberries across the floor. As I gathered them, I realised that blueberries were the last things you had eaten, days before, your jaundiced fingers picking them up one by one.

I left in Solomon's car. There were Christmas lights in the streets. A white spot on his neck. The keys to my flat in Stoke Newington were in my coat pocket and still fitted into the two locks on the blue front door. I still knew all the actions: twisting the keys and hearing the metal tongues of the locks draw back, pushing the door, walking in. I stood in the doorway of the bedroom. It was cold. My swimming things were on the radiator where I'd left them a week before.

Solomon opened tinned soup and put it in the micro-wave. I fell asleep on the sofa listening to it turn. His lips against my forehead, gentle and dry, shocked me awake and he placed the bowl into my hands. Our sheets smelled of detergent when we got into bed. Solomon touched my hair, smoothing it over the pillow. Once we turned the lamp off, it was him who cried in the dark.

And then it was the next day.

Harriet called from Canada. Her voice slightly hollowed by the distance. It was a different time there.

'I'm so sorry,' she said.

After she hung up, I got down on the floor and cleaned it, working from the kitchen sink through the three small rooms of the flat. Then I polished it all and lay down on top of it on my belly and sobbed and screamed into my hand until the doorbell went with flowers wrapped in printed cellophane with a white card stapled to the side: *From Sean.* Orange lilies from Solomon's dad, though the two of them hadn't spoken in months. I held them against my body for a long time by the sink.

I sat in the flat with Solomon, my finger tracing the wine stain on the arm of the sofa. He recounted a night out with the boys that I had told him not to pull out of. How they had hugged him and asked about me. I imagined his friends in their thin jackets, smoking in the street. Saying, *Oh, mate.* Buying him a drink when they went back in, a quick sting of closeness between them, the relief of chang-ing the subject.

'Let's go away,' he said. 'When I get paid, we can go to Rome.'

I stared at the wall feeling un-brave. I thought of him sniffing cocaine off a world atlas and the moment when you turn your phone on after a flight and any bad news might await you.

'I don't want to go to Rome.'

'Or anywhere,' he said. 'Wherever. Cornwall.'

I looked at him. A strand of hair had escaped his ponytail and hung at the side of his face. He seemed unreal, close but not touching me, and yet this person carried a possible version of my life. Here he was, holding it out like an object, trying to pass it into my palm.

'Emily,' he said, 'I love you.'

A silence.

He put his hand on my leg.

Then I said, 'I love you too.'

I did not say, *I think I might wish it was you.*

That January, I returned to university and sat in a black plastic seat, took a pen from my bag and began writing notes across a lined page. Everything was strange. But it was also as it had been before. The faces and actions were ones that I knew. I sat beside Yusuf. He had phoned me one afternoon in the holidays and said that his mother had also died. He had never mentioned her illness. After class, tears fell from my eyes as I descended the stairs. Claire was coming up and she stopped to wipe them from my face, very gently, her index fingers travelling up my cheeks as if she were ushering them home into my eyes.

I returned to the counsellor in the basement of lamps and ferns.

'Did you love your brother?' he asked.

After our sessions, I would walk through Regent's Park, drugged by sadness. An elderly woman was often there. Her legs spindly in black tights, palm out, feeding peanuts to the birds. I would grow older, I realised. In two years and some months, I would be older than you had ever been. The thought was followed immediately by the need to know exactly when.

'Why is the date important?' the counsellor asked.

I told him, 'It will be the beginning of the real future.'

But the future was already happening then. The future is always happening, to all of us. It climbs in through our windows while we sleep.

The summer after you died, an email arrived for me from a man named Tobias Michael who lived in Florida. I did not know this man, but he said he was deeply sorry for my loss. I read it and reread it, trying to work out who he was. Just before he signed off, he said, *Your father really was a wonderful man.* I waited for a few days and then sent a message back saying he must have the wrong address. Someone had died, but it was my brother, not my father. *This is truly weird*, Tobias Michael replied. *My friend Emily has your exact name.* He had left the dot out of her email address. After that, I often thought about the Emily grieving far away with my exact name. Because of the time difference, one of us would always be awake, moving through the world with our person who was not there.

I finished my degree and moved house. I live in a flat now that you never came to. You never sat in its kitchen eating Turkish bread, wetting your little finger to gather the scattered sesame seeds from across your plate. I did not get a dog.

There are times when I am wracked by your absence. So full of absence that I feel my skin will break. I have imagined emptying the kettle over myself, a red pattern blooming across my skin. I have imagined stepping out into the freezing morning unclothed. But I also know, have maybe always known, that these are things I will not do. There is really only so much space for drama, and when it happens, it happens very quietly in warm rooms with a kind female doctor who nods and takes your hand. After that, there are only the pathetic acts of violence against the self: standing under the kitchen light eating yellow strings of pickled cabbage until the whole jar is gone and the stomach is swollen and sore.

And there is happiness.

Sometimes I pause and put one hand softly over the other hand or touch my fingertips very lightly to my throat and feel a floating feeling. I smile. I did not know, until a happy segment of future arrived, that happiness waited for me intact. I am only partway into the future and so much remains to be seen. But one strange thing is that however much future happens, you never feel any further away. I was so afraid that you would sink into the past, down and out of sight like something dropped into the sea. But you don't. Not a miracle exactly but a glitch in the expected.

I have photographs. You in your long coat. You shaking a conductor's hand. You making pancakes with your friend, the girl who plays the harp. There are 486 pictures of you on Facebook. And there are the pictures pulled from developing fluid, our faces forming on the paper as it dried. *There was a person here*, they say. *There was once a person called Joe in the world.*

Emily & Edward

2015

Today, I woke, aged twenty-five years, nine months and five days.

My body was there as always. Teeth and the taste of my breath inside my mouth. I went into the kitchen and drank water. The tiles were smooth under my feet. I rinsed the glass and turned it upside down to dry. Then I went to King's Cross and boarded a train.

At Scarborough, Grandad stood waiting at the end of the platform, a loosely closed umbrella in one hand, Degas' ballerinas folding in on each other, slick with rain. He was tall, unhunched, his feet planted evenly on the concrete. Beside him stood a dark green shrub in a square pot. He saw me and slid his other hand from his pocket, lifting it to wave. I returned the wave as I walked toward him. He moved toward me smiling. Brown trousers and a green jumper. Inside my mind, you whispered, *He looks like a Christmas tree*, behind your hand. Inside my mind, I laughed with you quietly, conspirators at the dinner table, finding him both familiar and mysterious, and the two combining to make him not quite real. It was dim inside the station. Above us, metal girders crossed in the vaulted roof. I passed beneath the white circle of the hanging clock.

'Shall we hug?' he said.

I hugged him, and we left the platform through a stone arch.

Push of the pavement through our heels, knees, into our thighs. We walked up, heading to the castle above the town. Grandad did not seem out of breath. He told me about the friend who drove him to choir and how he fixed things in exchange: a broken radio, a smashed vase, a shoe coming loose from its sole. We passed houses with lattice windows and gnomes, severe terraces painted the gentle colours of baby blankets and cakes. Then the streets became grass.

On the hill, someone had lashed a small wooden cross to a tree with wire. It had a paper poppy in the centre and was bound to a clutch of dead flowers. I told him that you had gone to a memorial the month before you died. For Armistice. You had stood in the crowd in your long black coat, jaundiced and furling in at the edges but approximately young and strong, standing out among the old boys, who were slow to bend and place their flowers on the ground. You had told me that you felt close to all those dead young men. Grandad nodded and we walked on to the ruin.

When you and I were little, we could slip out of ourselves there and play a game called History. *Hand me my quiver!* you would yell, running to Grandad for arrows as enemies scaled the cliffs. Our grandparents sat on the bench and passed us invisible things. Draw back the bow.

Watch the arrow discharge. The dog all anticipation, then sprinting hard. Once, a stick landed in the ground, pointing up at an angle, and she skidded onto it. The tip cut her throat. Blood in her fur and us guilty, as if by calling it an arrow we'd made it sharp.

We sat down together on the bench and I took an orange from my bag, dug my thumb into the centre and began to peel.

Do you remember, you asked me, one day in hospital, *my party when Dad peeled an orange and there was an apple inside?* I told you that I did. I did not say, *Joe, that was my party*.

The orange scent released and covered my hands. Pith caught in my fingernails. I handed half to Grandad. I told him that I was older than you. Again, he nodded. And I knew why I had come here: to speak those words to a person who would be able to hear them. Who would not need explanation of who you were. Who would also not begin to sob. Our mother wept easily and spoke of medical procedures at any mention of your name. As if steps could be retraced and corrected. Our father was so slight. He had shrunk to bone without you. Hollows between the bones of his neck. His body broke my heart.

Grandad told me that Grandma had been seven years older than him, though that fact was put away and rarely taken out during their life together. It was embarrassing then, he said, for women to be older than their husbands. But she had died at seventy-three. He had passed through that age to become the older one at last. I didn't know how old he was. Salt wind trembled the grass around our bench. I apologised for not knowing. He told me: seventy-nine.

We walked down toward the sea. Gravity in our shins. I had never realised Grandma was older than him, and my ignorance almost felt pleasant, as if a small part of me was still a child. I knew that she had been divorced when they met. You had told me this long ago, having somehow discovered it one night when I had already been sent off for my earlier bedtime. I was incredulous then, finding it almost impossible to imagine her inside another life, another family. But now, I imagined it easily. For families are not fixed objects. People come and go, and she had almost walked cleanly past the life that would create us.

On the beach, I removed my clothes, my swimming costume underneath, and laid them over his arms. He said he would be my lifeguard. I turned and walked away from him over the sand, which was tight beneath my feet. The water lay flat and placid. I had checked the tides. The sea lapped my ankles. Further along the beach, I saw a white dog running over the sand. No, a white plastic bag, being carried and thrown and caught by the wind. I thought of the book of photographs our father had made for you in which all the things looked like other things. He had called it *Sometimes It All Looks Completely Different*. I owned it now.

I walked in deeper, up to my calves. The water touched the backs of my knees. My thighs and stomach. I remembered the blue of the sea in Spain. Standing in it, imagining the future, as if I knew the future would come.

In the almost year between your diagnosis and your death, I used to walk down the street saying, *And he lived*. Muttering the words quietly to the world. Miracles close, tempting as knives. I thought then that I could protect you by practising how I was going to tell it once it was over. But it failed.

There are so many living things. The world is full of them and so is the sea. But you are something else now. Something I am supposed to call memory. I pictured you, a boy again, climbing onto my back, your feet locking at my waist. Off we charged into the sea. The world is so full of those who aren't in it. Is it memory that sends us out into the ocean, up to our knees, waists, necks? We let it lap across our skin, collarbones, fingernails, a little on the tongue, on all our breakable parts. That urge to look at something so big that we can never get it into our vision all at once.

I tipped you backwards with a splash. I lay forward into the water. Shock of it hitting the flesh round my heart. I swam for a while then placed my feet down and walked toward Grandad standing on the beach. He adjusted my clothes into one hand so that he could wave. I waved back. It occurred to me, for a moment, to imagine you, old, waiting for me on the beach. You had always looked like him. Something in the bones of your faces.

Here I am, in the real future, I thought.

The other future hovered near me, as it often did. The future that would never be. You getting older. Twenty-eight. Thirty. Forty-one. Musicians playing music you had written, lifting instruments to their chins or mouths or holding them in front of their chests. Light dancing over the flutes. Or perhaps it would have never quite come off and you would become a glum failure. Either way, in that future we sat in our parents' kitchen and talked into the night.

Somewhere else, you got to fall asleep in someone's arms. His chest against your back in a bright white bedroom without any mess, without any death. I couldn't see his face, but you could feel his heart. Feeling of someone sleeping behind you and their body stirring, their cock stiffening against the base of your back. You tipping up your hips and pulling them close. *I am awake too*, the movement said. *I am awake. Come into me.* Somewhere you would have a cat. And somewhere you would look into a mirror one morning and see a wrinkle forming, your face creasing from use. It would be at the mouth or between the eyebrows, a line of concentration. Perhaps you would rub in creams, like a man I saw once in a department store, shyly asking at a counter for advice, putting air quotes round '*anti-ageing*', embarrassed to care. I thought about your future all the time. And it was funny to think that all that future was actually the past.

Grandad applauded as I returned to him. I spun my hair into a rope and squeezed some of the water onto the sand. I was shivering; my knuckles were white. He passed me my towel and I did my best to dry off and dress. The salt would curl my hair.

When I was ten, Grandma plugged her curler into the socket in the caravan and cooked ringlets into my hair, counting out the spirals as she released them. In the other room, you performed a piece just for Grandad – Küffner, I think – though of course we could hear you through the plywood wall. That night we went to a restaurant, because, they said, we were now both old enough. All evening, I kept touching the curls. They were crunchy with hairspray. We sat at the table in our pairs. You and me on one side, the tablecloth draping over our thighs, him and her on the other. Me opposite her. You opposite him. A memory sat coiled inside the memory. You much younger. Maybe six, on a white plastic chair in our garden. Straggles of long hair round your face. For months you had refused to have it cut, then one afternoon let Grandad do it with a pair of ordinary scissors. You held the underside of the seat as the dark strands fell past your ears into the grass.

Grandad gave me his coat. We left the beach. Up the stone beach steps and onto the seafront. We passed the sweet shop and the joke shop and Zoltar, the mannequin fortune teller in his glass case.

Then we floated, away from the water and into the streets of the town. Soft fingers stroked the skin above my heart. I loved the streets and the shining colours of the shops. The bodies. People glowed with gaps. The space where a baby had been. The space where a kidney had been. The space left slack where they took out the tumour. Sea water leaked from my hair as we moved through all the people and the dead. All the dead carried very gently from place to place. An old man with a brother on his back, draped across his shoulders like a coat. A woman with a shimmering child, its arms round her neck and knees resting on her hip bones. A man with a tattooed face holding the arm of a friend, quietly bearing her forward where he went, whispering into her hair. The cheap brooch pinned through a cardigan, touched sometimes to make sure it hadn't fallen off. The letter scratched into a table. The picture in a purse. The way he held his mug, hand round the body of it, the handle hanging free, just like his mother had. A young man wearing two wedding rings – his own and his father's – echo of a machine accident. The tyre burn on the road and the wilting bunch of flowers taped to a post. Each and every life formed round an absence. Grandad was beside me. And so were you. All the strangers smiled and knew our names.

Acknowledgements

My agent, Jennifer Hewson, for her enthusiasm, her patience and her insight. Jenny's belief in this book kept me going, and her guidance as I created the first drafts was invaluable. My generous and brilliant editor, Lettice Franklin, who both held this book sensitively and was ambitious for all that it could be. Isabelle Everington, Laura Collins and all at Weidenfeld & Nicholson who helped bring this book into being.

My teachers. Michael Nath at the University of Westminster, who guided me as I began to experiment with what would eventually become this novel and the University of Virginia's Creative Writing faculty, especially my advisor and friend, Jane Alison.

All who gave me writing space. Helen Grady and Mark Jackson for the dogs, stars and Spanish mountains. Catherine Clinton for Texas in August. Michelle Madsen for Larkspur, the houseboat in Mile End. Above all, my aunt Mair Harper, for offering many different spaces over the years, and for summoning me to get up after long days of writing to walk ankle-deep with her at dusk through the sea in France.

The late Betty Holme, who brought out the tea trolley and generously shared stories from her life in the name of research.

My friends. Write Club. My peers at UVA, especially Katie Rice and Cassie Davies, who emergency read sections for me when drafts were due, laughed with me and were never afraid of my grief, even when we were relative strangers. My allies in art and life, Rachel Lincoln and Daniel Holme. This book was painfully sad at times to write and to return to draft after draft. Many people stood at the edges of that experience, helping enormously and often unknowingly, just by being themselves and being kind.

My partner L, who arrived in my life, at last, for the final stretch.

David at Number 42.

'Craig', the student nurse, whoever and wherever you are. Long live compassion and long live the NHS.

My family, for their strong, fierce love and unwavering support. Nicki, Mike and Max. And most of all, thank you John Beecher. You always believed in my writing and you were with me every word. Brother, this book is for you.